A
PEACOCK
Speaks
AGAIN

DONALD J. PEACOCK

authorHOUSE®

AuthorHouse™
1663 Liberty Drive
Bloomington, IN 47403
www.authorhouse.com
Phone: 1 (800) 839-8640

Published by AuthorHouse   02/17/2016

ISBN: 978-1-5049-8031-9 (sc)
ISBN: 978-1-5049-8032-6 (e)

Library of Congress Control Number: 2016902683

Print information available on the last page.

CONTENTS

ACKNOWLEDGEMENT

T he author wishes to thank the people who helped him get into writing short stories and improving them, which led to getting them published. These include Nancy Pinard who taught the short story writing class at the University of Dayton's Institute of Lifelong Learning, and the Miami Valley writers group who's critiquing has improved my writing greatly.

Finally, a few other people to thank include my wife Rose, who puts up with my spending time on the computer with my writing and finally wound up being a published author herself. Also thanks to Julie Mitchell, Vice-President at the University of Dayton, who is in charge of Special Programs and Continuing Education and to Denise Quillen, who manages the daily interaction with students, liaisons, and moderators within the Institute of Lifelong Learning.

This book is a follow-on to my first book of short stories: 'A Peacock Speaks' published in 2012.

PUBLISHED YET?

"Welcome to the June meeting of our writer's group" Bill said as he looked around the room "It looks like we're all here. We can get on with our meeting. The first thing on our agenda is discussing genres for our future club contests. The top three choices are romance, kids, and science fiction. I understand in romance stories the current trend is to go very graphic. I don't think we need to go in that direction, although non-graphic hints can be very interesting. I would like to suggest we take those three categories and, over the next six months, have everyone write a short story in each one. You will have two months to write each story. At each second meeting be prepared to read your story and receive critiquing and comments on what you have written. Are there any suggested changes in the recommended topics?"

Quickly several hands went up. Currently the group of ten included six women and four men, all around the age of forty. Five of the women agreed they did not care much for writing science fiction. They wanted to make the third topic humor. Since the final count in the vote on this was five to five, it was decided to allow choosing between the two topics, science fiction or humor, as the third story.

Bill commented, "Now, if anyone could combine the two topics in one story they might well be ahead of the game. Do we have anybody who would like to try that?" Several hands went tentatively up prompting Bill to say, "We will look forward to that. Now our most important topic for today, which will probably take a lot of our time is how to get more of our stories published. There has to be a better way of doing this than just randomly sending them out to magazines and such. I've talked to people at the magazine 'Writing On' about the best way to get published in their publication. They said you just have to submit your story and if it is good enough it will be published.

We all know better than that. Everybody knows they have their favorites and they go with them first, and if they have a page or two left over to fill they might look at some of the other submissions. I don't know of a way around this problem, except to write enough stories and then self-publish a book and work hard selling it. With that procedure you might make a little bit of money and get known locally among your friends as an author. In the end I still think it's worth it."

Mary raised her hand. "I have an interesting, maybe funny, comment to make on all of this. My brother is a computer whiz. He can do anything with one. His latest interest is to see what websites he can hack into. Once in he tries to see how they operate and to look for potential ways to get some control of how they do things in their website. It is highly illegal and I probably shouldn't be telling you this. He has been successful in every website he has tried to hack into. He doesn't disturb or change anything in the website, he just observes what goes on. He really just enjoys his technical skills. But I was just thinking, it might be interesting to see if he could hack into the websites of some of these magazine companies that publish short stories. It would probably give us a lot of information we could use to get published more often."

Bill interjected, "I know hacking is illegal as all get out, but I think it is an interesting idea for our group to discuss. You're right, we could learn a lot about how these magazines really operate. Mary, maybe you could get your brother to come talk to our little group about this."

She replied, "I know he would enjoy doing that. I'll have him come to next month's meeting."

Finally the group got into discussing how and where they had been published. Seven of them had not yet been published so their part was in telling what kinds of stories they had submitted for publication, where they had been submitted, and repeating all of the comments they had received from editors telling them why they had been turned down.

It turned out to be a great meeting, thoroughly enjoyed by all of them. There were many comments about next month's meeting and its possible presentation on hacking into a publication's website. They all felt it would be very educational and interesting and all of them were already looking forward to it.

At the next month's meeting, as people settled in, Bill rapped on the table to call the meeting to order. The computer was all set up and ready to go. Bill made a few opening remarks, and then said, "I guess we can get directly into our program for this month. I would like to introduce John Harpell, who is going to show us some interesting things today. Everything is ready to go, John. The floor and the computer are all yours."

John walked to the front of the room, spent a few minutes telling the group all about himself. Then he went over to the computer, pulled out a flash drive and inserted it into one of the USB ports on the computer. He invited everyone to pull their chairs up behind him so they could better see what was happening as he started to download a couple of programs onto the computer. Then he activated one of the programs he had downloaded. As he started, he explained what he was doing and what they should see on the display.

He inserted the web address of the magazine into his program and hit enter. The program automatically started looking for passwords. After ten minutes it had found eight passwords and opened up many sections of the company's website. He then started browsing through all of the sections making notes as he went. He found the section which handled the outgoing mail and noted the address of the printer the magazine was sent to each month. He also made a note of the day of the month it usually went out. He then set up a capture program on the outgoing mail, which allowed him to put a hold on the magazine and to see the details that were in it. He told the group that from there he had full access and could make any changes he wanted before sending it on to the printer.

Bill spoke up at that point, "I can see a great opportunity in knowing all of this. We could replace one of their stories with one of ours and it would then go directly to the printer. The magazine would be printed and out for sale before anyone in the company would know about it."

Mary asked, "The editor of 'Writing On' probably gives the magazine a good look over when he receives the final printed copy. Wouldn't he raise a giant fuss about a story being changed without his approval?"

John stated, "I was looking at the management structure of the magazine and I saw they have two editors with equal duties and equal rights to make changes each month. That means a change could be made and probably the editors would assume that the change was made by the other editor at the last moment before the copy went out. By changing a story only every third or fourth month, you could probably go for two or three years, at least, without anyone catching on to what we are doing. I say, let's do it."

Bill responded, "Let's pick a story and give this a try next month. We can use a pseudonym for the author on this first try if we want to protect the true author from future reprisals."

"I think we should go ahead and use the author's real name so they can point to it as being published," Mary stated.

"Someone could get in real trouble if things go wrong. Would you like to volunteer a story for the first try?"

"I have a bunch of stories finished, so I could probably easily meet the number of words needed to replace one of their stories. Yes, I would like to go first."

"Are your stories good ones?"

"All of my stories are good. Trust me."

A month later Bill, John, and Mary met at John's house to make their first attempt at inserting a story. The information they had found indicated the magazine would be electronically forwarded to the publisher at 11:15 am exactly. They also knew the publisher was expecting to receive it before 11:30 am, so they had fifteen minutes to make the change and forward it.

At ten minutes after eleven John hacked in and set things up to intercept the magazine. At precisely fifteen minutes after eleven he had it on his computer and was prepared to go. He had five of Mary's stories so all he had to do was find out the word count of two or three of the stories in the digital magazine and match one of those with one of Mary's stories.

It took him less than two minutes to find a story that was a close match in length to one of Mary's. It then took him one and a half minutes to make the exchange and to check that nothing else was perturbed. Then he quickly forwarded the magazine to the publisher. Finally he logged out, turned off his computer and prepared to go home and wait for the printed magazine to come available, which usually took about five days.

A week later Bill found copies of the magazine in the local bookstore. He bought copies for himself and Mary and took them to the next writer's meeting. Mary's story had fit in very precisely and the change was not noticeable. John had also hacked into the magazines website and examined their e-mail. He did not find anything unusual in the e-mails. It appeared they had been completely successful.

Three months later they ran the same process with one of Bill's stories and again with apparent complete success. This went on every three months for three years, at which time the members of the writing group wanted a break. Also at this time they all agreed to go back to the normal process for publishing, which turned out to be a lot easier since all of them could now show a list of published stories.

THE WANNABE WRITERS

D an Vallenti, the group President, was the last one to show up for the monthly meeting. His excuse, "My wife needed something done," and took a seat at the end of the table.

The group had been meeting monthly at the library for a couple of years now with all of them hoping to make the big announcement they were going to get something published. Of the ten of them only one had managed to publish any of their writing. Getting a piece of fiction published in the current market was really tough, as they all were finding out.

"Not a problem," John Harrison said to Dan as he got out the agenda for this month's meeting. John had served as the secretary of the group from the time they had first formed. The truth was, nobody else wanted to do it, and John enjoyed doing it. The real truth was it fit in with his life style perfectly. He was a book keeper at a local company and enjoyed crawling through details both minor and major. His happiest days were when he could spend a few hours picking through the details of almost anything. Plus, he was good at it.

Dan Vallenti also enjoyed his job as the writing group President. It gave him a chance to direct people along with a feeling of power, which his regular job wouldn't allow. His regular job was, like John, a bookkeeper at a large company. The two of them approached their similar jobs in totally different ways, which is probably why they got along so well in the writing group.

John, reading from his list, said, "The first thing we need to do is go around the group and see if there are any comments or questions about last month's program. We'll start with Jim since he is seated at the foot of the table."

Without hesitation, going around the table, ten heads were vigorously shaking 'No'.

"The next point is 'Does anyone have anything to report about getting published or near published over the last month?"

Without hesitation, going around the table, ten heads were vigorously shaking 'No'.

"The third point is 'Has anyone started a new story or book in the last month?"

Without hesitation, going around the table, ten heads were vigorously shaking 'Yes'.

"Well it looks like reading new starts will take up most of this meeting. We'll limit the readings to one page for each one of us."

Groans erupted from every seat at the table.

"Those of us who did not bring their lunch plan on leaving to go to lunch. If you brought your lunch you can read to anyone who is here after that. I suspect it will be, at most, one person."

They started reading the one page of their new stories with three of them trying to read through a second page. All three of them were immediately cut off by Vallenti and their punishment was there would be no discussion of their work by the group.

"I warned you. One page only," chided Vallenti.

John Harrison broke in with, "Dan's President for another year and a half. At that point, I have a feeling he will be ready to pass the gavel to someone else."

The readings were followed by extensive, detailed discussion of what was needed for getting published. Finally someone mentioned the possibility of all of their new stories being published in one book. This way they might have better control of things. After more discussion, it was agreed the one book idea may be their best option. This was followed by more discussion concerning where each of them stood in finishing their story. Five were in final editing, three were three-fourths done writing, and two were just getting into writing their story. These last two estimated four months to being ready for final edit.

"Well, I think we have a reasonable schedule for our book to be ready. Next month we will look at places to submit the book for publishing," Dan said. "Now I'm going home. All of you can stay as long as you like."

Nine people followed him out the door and headed home to have lunch and work on their stories.

-- -- --

At the next monthly meeting Dan started the discussion of publishing and where to go to accomplish it. As discussion got started, John said, "We probably should see what kinds of stories are being written by each of us. This could have an impact on what we do. Let's start with our President and work our way around the room.

Dan started with, "I'm writing a story about a family trapped in the desert when their car overheats and destroys the radiator. I'm shooting for around forty pages and have twenty-five now."

They started around the table.

"I'm doing a non-fiction story about my family and growing up in Southern California. I'm looking at around thirty-five pages."

"I'll add in a fictional story about meeting a pair of mermaids living in Lake Erie. It will be about thirty pages and will be a very clean story in terms of a lot of water and the mermaids don't go topless.

The next one to speak was one of the pair of brothers in the group. "My story is a religious one. The basis of it is Jesus appearing in the halls of Congress while they are in session. The actions of the Congressmen make for some great humor. It'll be about fifty pages."

His brother spoke next with "Well, my story is an erotic one. It's about a naked supermodel appearing in Congress during a session discussing cutting all poor people out of all benefits. The humor in mine is around the Congressmen trying to get the supermodel to sit with them while they lay off government employees. I'm trying for about forty-five pages."

"My story is non-fiction. It is about my father working on a Top Secret project during World War I. I have all of the documentation on it, the results, and what it meant to the war effort. I'm expecting about fifty pages."

Next in line was John Harrison who commented, "We seem to have quite a variety of stories. Mine will add more variety. I'm working on a fantasy story. I have written a couple of them in the past, but this will be my longest one yet at around twenty-five pages. I have written the start and have an extensive outline of where I'm going with it."

Number eight in the lineup was Stephanie, the only female in the group. She spoke up, "I'm writing a very gentle love story based on my parents, the way they met, and where they fell in love. I have it about seventy-five percent written and am trying to decide how far in their lives to take it. My story will be either thirty-five pages or one hundred thirty five. At this time I'm going for the shorter one. My problem in writing it is I keep starting to cry. They both are gone now and I miss them terribly."

Next in line, at twenty-two, was the youngest one in the group. "Mine is a horror story. I have two ghosts, a dragon, an ogre, and a witch in it. I think it is going to approach seventy-five pages. I don't see any way to shorten it without damaging my story line."

Finally the oldest guy spoke up, "My story touches on a lot of the mentioned themes. It is about a senior couple who have lost their spouses. They meet at a Halloween party at the senior center. He invites her out for coffee and dessert after the party. Over the next few months they learn to love each other. They get married obviously, with full support from both of their families. This has nothing to do with my wife and I. We have been happily married for fifty-five years. I'm trying for about thirty pages overall."

-- -- --

At the third monthly meeting the main topic of discussion was 'The Book'. They all presented the status of their stories and everyone seemed to be on schedule for the chosen date for a final pulling together and overall edit. Then they got into what the lineup of the stories were going to be. It looked like they might even come to blows over this. President Dan finally proposed an order based on achieving a good mix of genres. Since he had put his own story in eighth place in the lineup, nobody could really argue with him, thus settling their major disagreement.

After struggling with rewriting, rewording, and editing, Dan commented "At last, I think we have this book where we want it. It really reads well and may be some of our best work."

They started looking through writing magazines, such as 'The Writer's Digest' and 'The Writer', to see if they could find a good place to submit it. The two latest issues of the magazines had a number of sites that looked like good possibilities. They had ten companies as possible places to submit the book. They finally selected the first two and began to ready it and put together the necessary information to meet the requirements for submission. After eight rejection notices, it was finally accepted by a lesser known publisher with a base in England.

Not long after publication the group received a call from a well known fiction writer saying he really liked their book and its variety of stories. He asked about joint authorship of a book of short stories. They all agree to try to do this realizing they now had a major project over the six months. They emailed back and forth on ideas and approaches to working with the well known author. They find acceptance for publication easy based on the famous author's name. The book eventually becomes a best seller and earns a large amount of money for the authors.

Giving a talk at a publishing conference Dan commented he had promised to buy the famous author a diamond wrist watch when they earned the first million dollars. He had to admit they weren't there yet.

WHAT'S THAT?

The male peacock was parading across the grassy shoreline, headed for the water to get a drink. He had many interests at the moment, among them water, food, female peacocks, whichever came first. All of a sudden something caught his eye. It was tall and pink and the peacock had never seen anything like that before. In actuality it was a pink flamingo that had been blown into the area out of its normal range by a wind storm and was just settling down from the wild experience and starting to look for food when the peacock came into view.

Both birds took protective stances and they stared at each other for over a minute, waiting to see who was going to do what. Finally the flamingo cautiously started to move down the shoreline away from the peacock. As it was moving away the peacock was watching closely and tentatively moving in the other direction looking for the best place to get a drink of water.

As they headed in opposite directions around the lake they assumed that was that and they would never see each other again. But they didn't realize the lake was only about one hundred yards across. Thus it wasn't long before they saw the distance between them growing shorter.

As they approached each other once again, each one went into their personal show-off actions. The peacock spread his tail and started strutting as well as any peacock ever had. The flamingo, not being much into strutting, tried to stand as tall as it could, giving a full display of beautiful pink feathers.

It was obvious that each one was trying to win the contest to see which was the prettiest and the most dominant.

As they finally started to get a little used to each other and realized that the other one was not dangerous, they settled down to dining, the peacock looking for insects in the grass and the flamingo going after small fish in the water's edge.

More time passed and they even came close enough to really check each other out. This included even standing wing to wing as they watched a couple of hawks circling overhead. They finally decided the hawks weren't big enough to bother them and went back to looking for food. Every so often they would approach each other and spend some time in close proximity. They seemed to be not only getting used to each other but beginning to truly enjoying each other's company.

After another three weeks the two birds appeared to be inseparable. They were always together and local people were driving to the lake just to see them wandering around together. People were starting to speculate on whether it was possible for two different species to create babies. There was a great deal of discussion on what the babies might look like. The general guess was a long legged bird that is all pink except for the tail which would be huge, spreading over a large area, and be pink, green, and blue in color with spots of red mixed in.

There was a lot more guessing as to what they could be called. The favorite two choices were peamingo or flamock.

Finally, one day, an ornithologist dropped by to see what was going on with the two birds. He took a long look at the two and announced, "Babies, what babies? These are two male birds."

BIRD CRAZY

John stood in front of the peacock area of the ornithology section of the zoo. He enjoyed watching any of the exotic birds in their collection, but he most enjoyed watching the peacocks. Currently, the male peacocks were busy strutting around with their giant tails spread, trying to interest the females in some extracurricular activity. The females were busy enjoying the lunch the zookeeper had just deposited in their area.

As John stood there, a very lovely young lady walked up to the owl display about twenty feet away and started making notes on a pad of paper. As she started writing John moved a little closer and finally asked, "Hello. I've seen you here in this area before. Are you an ornithologist?"

She looked over at him, saw a tall, well-built young man and decided he was reasonably harmless, and answered, "Not yet. My graduation is in six months. I'm working toward a job here at the zoo, specializing in the many species of owls. They are the most magnificent birds on earth."

"If you think that let me introduce you to the peacocks. They're right over here," was John's reply.

"I know where they are located", she answered with a 'go away' tone in her voice. I am quite familiar with all of the birds in this zoo. Now if you will excuse me I have some work to do."

With that she returned to her notes on the owls.

Not to be deterred, John again spoke up, "My name is John Peacock. I received my degree in ornithology last year and now work here at the zoo. I think you're the dedicated type of person we need."

She gave him a strange look and said, "If that isn't a pickup line, it's very nice of you. Is that really your name?"

"Yes it is and I have the genealogy charts to prove it. I very much mean what I said", he replied with a grin, "but if you want to join me for dinner some evening it would be fine with me."

"Let me think about it. Now if you'll excuse me I need to finish this. It's part of my graduation thesis."

As he turned to head back to the peacock area he tossed over his shoulder, "How often do you come here?"

"About every other day," she responded.

John was a bit surprised she told him that much. Then as an afterthought he asked, "What's your name?"

After a momentary hesitation, "It's Olivia Lang. Olivia Wanda Lang."

Finally he decided he had better get back to gathering information for the article he was writing on peacocks. He had quite a few pictures to get and considerable writing to do in order to meet his deadline.

Three hours later, back at home, as he was digging things out for supper, still thinking of what Olivia had said, when it struck him. Her initials, O. W. L., spelled 'owl'. He started to laugh. She was working on her initials and he was working on his last name. Owls and peacocks. Peacocks and owls. He was laughing so hard he had to sit down. He hadn't laughed this hard since the time he had made his brother look so foolish in front of his then girlfriend. His brother had started to work him over about it, but John was laughing so much his brother had to start laughing also.

He remembered how the prank, in the end, had created a greater friendship with his brother than had existed before, and he suddenly had a pleasant feeling about the owl and the peacock.

Four days later John was back at the peacock exhibit taking the final pictures he needed for his article, which he was hoping to publish in a nationally recognized magazine, when Olivia came walking up to the owl area with her camera and notepad. She started taking some notes and then raised the camera for some pictures. She sighted in, focused, and pushed the button. Nothing happened. John saw her start checking the camera. When she finally realized the battery needed charged, she mumbled a couple of words under her breath and started to put the camera back in her purse.

John had glanced over, seen all of this, and came over to her, "What's the matter with the camera?"

"It apparently needs charging. I need these pictures for tomorrow to finish a first cut of my thesis."

John said, "I have a suggestion. Why don't I loan you my camera. After you're done I'll take it home, download the pictures, and email them to you. It would be an easy solution to your problem."

"That would be very nice of you. Here let me give you my email address."

She tore a page out of her notepad, wrote down her email address and gave the page to him.

He commented, "I'll send the pictures to you before eight-thirty tonight. Does that work for you?"

"Yes it does. I really appreciate your doing this," Olivia responded.

"By the way," John continued, "I figured out what your initials spell and I understand why you are studying owls. Do other people ever figure this out?"

"Oh yes. In high school they nicknamed me 'Owl' so I don't usually tell people my middle name. It took me three years to get them to call me 'Olivia'. I hated being called 'owl'.

"That's funny. In high school they started to try calling me 'birdy', but I brought it to a quick stop since I was already six feet four inches tall. They got the idea quickly. Here is my camera. I'll show you how to use it. It's very easy."

He showed her the focus button and the shutter release and said, "If you have a problem with it I'll be right over here. I plan on being here for another hour or two."

Olivia shot several dozen pictures over the next hour and a half. When she was finished, she walked over to John and handed him the camera.

"I have my pictures now. Thank you for helping me out. I'll look forward to receiving the pictures this evening. Now I need to get back to my notes."

She walked back to the owl exhibit, while John put his camera away and headed to his car.

Three hours later, after John had fixed himself an out of the box meal, he got busy emailing the pictures to Olivia. He couldn't help but notice she had taken some outstanding pictures of the owls, including the Great Horned Owl and the Barn Owl.

He then attached the pictures to four email messages telling Olivia she had taken some excellent pictures. As a footnote to the message he added, 'Looking forward to seeing you again at the zoo'.

The next morning John had a response to his email and she again thanked him for resolving her camera problem.

She added that she would be at the zoo on Friday, three days away, and she would have the first draft of her thesis to show him.

John quickly emailed back to her saying that he looked forward to seeing her writing and he would have the notes and pictures on his article to show her. He also said his first draft was about a month away.

Friday finally rolled around and John happily headed for the zoo, ostensibly to get more peacock pictures, but in reality to meet with Olivia again.

At the zoo, John went directly to the owl exhibit but Olivia was nowhere in sight. He wandered through the zoo and finally found her in front of the songbird exhibit and walked up behind her and said in a teasing voice, "These are awfully small to be owls. Are they in disguise?"

Olivia chuckled, "You know better than that. These are some of the prettiest birds around, particularly the cardinals and goldfinches. They're so interesting to watch."

"I agree. I spend quite a lot of time here in this area and greatly enjoy it," was John's response.

Olivia continued, "I also enjoy watching the wild turkeys in the wooded area north of here about five miles. There are quite a lot of them there."

"They have a turkey exhibit here. Have you seen it?"

Olivia replied, "I thought the turkey section was the one by the owl exhibit. The one with the big birds spreading their tails and strutting around."

With a smile John asked, "Would you like to see my turkey walk?" He proceeded to flap his elbows and wiggle his rear end while making gobbling sounds, and strutted back and forth. Olivia stood there and laughed so loud the other zoo visitors kept looking at them.

Then John continued, "I still think the peacocks are the most fascinating birds in this zoo and also the prettiest. Owls are so bland in color."

"I disagree. If you take the time to watch them, the gradations of color in the owls are magnificent. Their coloration is great for hiding when they are hunting small mammals, and it stands out when mating season is here. The peacocks could never hide anywhere, and their coloration is obscenely bright during mating season."

John could only say, "I think we both have good points. All species of birds have their own variations in color and actions. That's why it is so great observing and studying them. That's why I've made it my career."

Olivia replied, "I agree with you. It is why I'm making my career the study of birds. Maybe we can work together in the future."

"That's a great idea. Now have you reconsidered having lunch with me sometime?"

"I'm sure I would enjoy lunch with you. I can probably fit it in my study schedule. Tuesday's are the best days for me."

"Well, that's great. Next Tuesday for lunch." They exchanged phone numbers, then John said, "I think we have everything settled", and leaned over and gave Olivia a very gentle kiss, which she didn't object to happening.

WHY ME? WHY NOW?

As the Chevy went by the parked police car, the two policemen in the car sat up straight and stared. They could see the driver of the Chevy was an elderly man, very obviously elderly. But doing thirty-five miles per hour down the interstate was certainly an attention getter. The two policemen looked at each other, turned on the flashing red lights, and pulled onto the highway in 'hot' pursuit. Well not very hot since the elderly driver was going so slow.

They quickly pulled up behind the slow Chevy, lights and sirens blaring. The driver still acted as if he neither heard nor saw anything unusual. The police changed lanes and pulled up beside the car. The driver continued on so the police car sped up to forty-five miles per hour and moved over in front of the Chevy. They then proceeded to slowly reduce speed. The police began to realize it was going to be a difficult stop so they called for backup. In less than five minutes another police car showed up and assumed a position behind the Chevy to help stop it.

Immediately the Chevy started to change lanes to the left. The lead police car quickly moved over to stay in front of it while still slowly decreasing speed. At that point, a third police car appeared and assumed a position beside the leading police car. This way they had two lanes covered in front of the slow car. They were also getting a long line of cars behind them. It seemed, as the cars behind them could get past, the drivers of those cars were either enjoying the show that was going on or cursing everything around them.

The Chevy finally pulled over to the berm and came to a stop with police cars ahead of, beside, and behind it, with the fourth side being against a guard rail. All four of the policemen got out of their cars and walked to the Chevy, covering both sides of it. When they reached the side windows, the driver, starting to look panicked, rolled down the window on his side, looked at the policeman standing there and asked, "What's wrong? Is there an accident up ahead?"

"Not yet," replied the policeman. "That's what we are trying to prevent. Can I see your driver's license and proof of insurance?

The man fumbled with his wallet, pulled out his driver's license and handed it to the policeman.

He noted the driver's name was George Baker. He asked, "Do you know what speed you were going?"

"Not really. Was I exceeding the speed limit?"

"No. Quite the reverse. You were driving at about half the speed limit."

"Well, I don't see that really being a problem. I think you guys should spend your time catching the speeders, not the ones driving under the speed limit."

"The problem, sir, is someone driving the speed limit or higher might rear end you and create great problems for you and us. Your family doesn't really want to attend your funeral, do they?"

"I don't care any more. My wife of seventy-five years has just left me for a younger man. I'm so upset I can't see straight."

"Well, it was obvious from the way you were driving. I see by your driver's license that you are ninety-five years old."

"I'm ninety-five as of last month. We've been married for seventy-five years. The other man is seventy-seven years old. Almost a youngster."

"How old is your wife, if I may ask?"

"She is ninety-three. We had a perfect marriage until last year. Then she decided she didn't want to have sex anymore."

The officer tried to suppress a smile. "I think you are getting beyond the information I need, but why did she go for a younger man instead of an older one?"

"She didn't know any guys older than me, so she went for one she might be able to train."

The policeman got a strange look on his face and then turned away, trying not to burst into peals of laughter. At last he got control of himself and turned back to the ninety-five year old driver. "You'll ride with me back to your place, we'll have your car towed. I see by your driver's license you live about a mile from my station. Is that agreeable?"

"Well, I think I'm perfectly capable of driving. I was headed to the Mall to get some things. Can we make a stop first?"

"I'm afraid not. We'll take you straight home. Your car will be held at the station. You can talk to them tomorrow about getting it back."

"Why. What was your name again? I want to talk to your supervisor about all of this."

"My name is Harry Peterson and he will be informed after I write this up."

The tow truck drove up at last and the driver started hooking up the Chevy. While he was doing this, he talked to Officer Peterson about where to take the car and if the elderly man had a ride to where he needed to go. After getting all of this information, he took off with the Chevy as Peterson helped the elderly man into his cruiser to drive him home.

The next morning everybody in the police station had heard about the driver traveling thirty-five mile per hour on the interstate. They were all waiting for him to show up at the station to talk to the supervisor and try to get his car back. By afternoon everybody had given up on seeing him. Two days later he arrived, walked into the supervisor's office and sat, "We need to talk. I need my car. Right now!"

"That's not going to happen just yet. There are a few things to settle. The first thing is to have you retake the driver's license tests, the whole thing, including some health checks and an eye exam."

"My license is valid. I don't have to do all those tests."

"Yes you do since I have just called Judge Johnson and requested he revoke your current license. He agreed to it being done."

"I'll talk to the Mayor about you. He'll take my side."

"He's always taken my side in the past, so don't get your hopes up. I'm sure that won't change. When do you want to schedule your tests?"

"You're just picking on me. I object."

"Object all you want but let's go ahead and schedule the exams."

"I can't do them before next Wednesday. You think you've won, don't you."

"Well, I think that's becoming more and more apparent. Do you need a ride home.?"

"No. I'll catch the bus, thank you."

George got up and strode out of the police station muttering to himself. After he was gone, the Supervisor called the BMV office and scheduled Mr. Baker for 1:00 pm on Wednesday. He then asked his secretary to get word to him about the time of his appointment. Finally he couldn't control himself and broke out into laughter over the whole thing.

Come Wednesday, George showed up at the BMV at 12:45 pm and took a number. At 1:20 his number was called and he was taken into a side room to begin his eye and reflex testing. These checks showed everything to be acceptable as long as he wore glasses while driving. George was taken outside for the actual driving test. After another half hour wait he was introduced to the man who was going to oversee this part of the testing. They proceeded to George's car which was being held on the lot. Twenty minutes later George had passed all parts of the exam and had his drivers license returned to him.

During the testing he talked about the problem that had caused everything. The tester pursued this a bit to ensure it would not be a factor in George's driving in the future.

George said he belonged to two senior centers and he had plans to go to them over the next couple of weeks to look for a younger woman to replace is wife. He said he would be looking for someone in the range of seventy-five to seventy-seven. According to him the senior centers usually had a goodly number of widows and he had high hopes of finding someone. He further said he was not rich, but he was fairly well off and that should be a help in finding someone.

The man in charge of his testing asked him why he had been driving so slowly.

The answer he got was, "I was so mad at my wife for leaving me that I couldn't get my attention focused on my driving."

"You shouldn't have been driving at that time."

"I fully understand that now."

The man who had handled the testing couldn't think of any kind of reply to all of this so he released George's car keys to him, said goodbye and good luck and went back into the building shaking his head.

George got into his car, started it, and headed for home. When he arrived home he saw the front door was standing open. He stopped in the driveway, climbed out of the car, and cautiously started in the front door. As he entered the living room he saw his wife sitting on the sofa watching television.

"What are you doing here," he sputtered. "I thought you were gone for good.

"Bill was way too young for me. The first thing he wanted to do was go to his place. I knew what he had in mind, so I decided to give this marriage another chance. But you need to remember that you are on monthly probation.

As George's jaw fell, his wife got up and went to the fridge to get a glass of iced tea.

The only thought in George's head was Why me? Why now?

HELLO THERE

Entering John's apartment, Evelyn could hear the shower running so she knew where to find him. She headed to the bathroom, quietly pushed open the door and crept over to the shower, "Hi John. How are you today?"

John jumped about two feet high, whirled around facing the shower door, "Evelyn. What are you doing here? Why are you here while I'm in the shower? What do you want?" He tried desperately to shield himself with his hands.

She laughed. "I'm seventy-five and not interested in what you're wearing or not wearing. I've got way too many other priorities. I just came by to tell you we urgently need you at the church this afternoon to go over the annual expenses to see where we stand and to start some initial planning for next year."

He sighed, "I don't know how both of us wound up on the same Board at church. Maybe I definitely need to move to another Board." He moved around behind the foggy shower door still trying to conceal himself. Evelyn smiled at both his comment and his nervousness.

"You can't do that. You love working with me."

"Just tell me what time the meeting is and get the hell out of here."

"The meeting is scheduled for three p.m."

"Get out. Get out right now." The sound of his voice echoed around the tiled room.

"OK, OK, I'm leaving. See you at three o'clock."

"Only if I can't scrape up something else to do at that time."

"Remember, three o'clock."

"Out! Out! Out! Damn it, out!" he yelled, his voice rising with each word.

Evelyn waved goodbye with her middle finger and headed to the front door, "By the way, you should always lock your front door, especially when you take a shower. I'll lock it on my way out so none of your other girl friends can come to visit you."

She laughed and pulled the door shut but the continuous tirade of profanity coming from the bathroom could still be heard when she walked out the front door.

After Evelyn left, John finished his shower, got dressed, and glanced at the clock. He saw he had six hours to pull things together and get to the meeting. He had the financial data in order, he just needed to review it. Right now, though, his mind wasn't on the numbers but rather how to get even with Evelyn for what she just pulled. He also made a mental note to ensure he locked the front door after bringing in the morning paper in the future.

He put the breakfast dishes in the dishwasher and pulled out the financial information. As he reviewed it, his mind kept slipping back to Evelyn and his embarrassing morning.

Later that afternoon John walked into the empty meeting room, noticing he was the first one there. He picked up the latest information on the church finances, sat down at the table and started reviewing the update. It showed they were right on target for the year.

Minutes later Evelyn and three men entered the room. They greeted John and took a seat at the table.

"Well," Dave, the Board Chairman, commented, "we are still short three people, but they should be here soon. Meanwhile let's look at the current data sheet and see if we find any potential problems."

"I've looked it over and everything seems to be in great shape," John said.

"I don't spot any problems after a quick look," Dave replied, "Let's just hope all of our church members maintain their pledges and, if so, we may have a little extra money for some needed repairs."

"That would be nice," commented Evelyn, "as we do have a few unfunded repairs on the list.".

The other three Board members filed into the room and they held further discussion of the new data. Soon everyone agreed things were, at this point, in good order. Next they discussed how soon they needed to finalize next year's budget.

"You realize, Evelyn," Dave said, "my term as Chairman ends in four months. I'm going to suggest to the Executive Board they appoint you as Chairman."

"I'll think about it but I really have a lot on my plate right now."

"Oh, I know you can handle it. Go ahead and accept. You're strong enough to have a really good impact."

"I'll take it under advisement but I still have a couple of months to decide."

As the group broke up, Evelyn went over to John and said, "I really would like to apologize for walking in on you in the shower and scaring you like I did."

John replied, "I accept your apology," but he still felt some sort of revenge was necessary.

On her way out the door she turned back and asked John how old he was and if he had ever been married, totally catching him off guard.

He thought she was a little presumptuous. "I'm thirty-five and I haven't yet met the right lady."

"Thanks. I was just curious," she said as she turned and headed out the door.

As everybody was leaving the meeting room John was still plotting some way to get even with her. He hadn't yet come up with a plan, but he'd give it more thought. He decided he needed to go to the fitness center and get a good workout knowing he would feel a lot better afterwards. He stopped at the drugstore for some water and then went on to the gym. Grabbing his gym bag, which he always kept in the car, he went into the building.

He checked in and headed to the dressing rooms. As he walked along he thought about the church budget and tried to think of possibilities of how they could get some extra money for needed repairs.

He entered the back area where the dressing rooms were, not paying attention, and then he turned and entered the nearest dressing room.

Suddenly he heard someone gasp. He looked up and there stood Evelyn with nothing on, not even a towel. She stood frozen for about two seconds and then rushed over to a towel rack, grabbed one, and held it in front of herself. She turned back to John. "John! What the hell are you doing in the women's dressing room? You better get out of here now!", she said as she fumbled with the towel trying to cover herself.

John was rooted in total shock, staring at Evelyn. Then he turned and, scurried out of the women's dressing room. He was totally embarrassed by what had happened. Instead of going to the men's dressing room he rushed out of the building as quickly as he could, jumped into his car and drove home. Once there he grabbed a couple of beers from the fridge, sat down in the living room, and gulped them down quickly trying to recover.

After the two beers, he settled down enough to call for a pizza delivery so he wouldn't do any drunk driving to top everything off.

******

A month later, as the time for the board meeting approached, John was nervous about attending and seeing Evelyn again, but finally decided he felt he had to contribute his ideas for the budget problem. With a lot of trepidation he headed to the meeting. At the church he went to the meeting room and sat at the opposite end of the table from Evelyn.

Throughout the meeting the group discussed everyone's input about the budget with all of them liking John's ideas of where to tighten up to free up money. He was glad he came after all. At that point the meeting started to break up. Evelyn caught John before he left and said they needed to talk.

The two of them sat down at the table and, with some hesitation and embarrassment, got into a lengthy discussion of everything that had happened.

Finally each one apologized to the other and promised to do their best to make sure such things never happened again. They then hugged and went out the door to go home.

The following Sunday, after church services, John was making his way back to the gathering room when Dave called him over and introduced him to a young lady named Marian Connors. It turned out she had just moved back to town and was going to become a member of their church.

John was immediately struck by her beauty. The more they talked, the more he realized how intelligent she was. After a while she admitted to having a PhD in physics and a B.S. in archeology. John began to feel somewhat intimidated, but at the same time Marian started to understand how relaxed he was while talking with her. They stood and chatted for half an hour, covering an array of topics of mutual interest.

At that point Evelyn approached them, "I see you've met my granddaughter John. She's moving in with me until she can find a place."

"Your granddaughter? You only had a son, how come Marian's last name is not the same as yours?"

"Our last names are not the same because Gramma married a second time after my grandfather passed away." Marian said. "Her original married last name was the same as mine."

They all walked into the gathering room. Later, before parting, John got Marian's cell phone number. John and Evelyn stayed for a while longer to continue talking about the Board business.

"On a personal note," John asked, "do you mind if I call your granddaughter about going out with me?"

"I have no problem with you asking her out." she said with a twinkle in her eye. "Are you going to tell her we have seen each other completely naked?"

"I will never tell her and I suggest you shouldn't either."

"I heartily agree. Now I need to head home and help Marian get settled in. See you next week."

"Okay. And Evelyn..."

"Yes?", she replied turning to look at him one last time.

I'll be keeping my front door locked, "he said grinning at her, "and see you in church."

RACING TO THE FUTURE

B orn ten days apart, they grew up as if they were twins instead of next door neighbors. They were always together. As a pair they attended all family affairs, both his and hers. They always had a lot of fun together, laughing and kidding. The racing competition started when they were eight years old. Up until then they were just having fun together. In the end they found they thoroughly enjoyed competing against each other as well as having fun while they competed.

-- -- --

"Come on, Mary. Once around the block."

"Oh Bill, the whole block? We usually just walk along this side. Dad doesn't want us to go too far out of sight. We're only eight years old."

"One side isn't long enough. Besides, we're big enough to go the whole block. Come on. A real race. The whole block."

At the command they both took off running as fast as they could. On the first two sides the lead switched back and forth with neither of them gaining any real advantage.

As they rounded the second corner Mary said, "I'm keeping up with you Bill. I can still win this race."

On the third side, Bill pulled about two feet ahead and slowly continued pulling away. As they approached the fourth turn, Bill looked back and yelled, "Watch this. I'm going to turn it on." At the final corner Mary called out, "I'm quitting. You always find some way to win at almost anything whenever we compete."

"I'm the boy. I'm supposed to win."

"Well, I can still beat you at checkers."

"Aw. Checkers is just a game. A race is what really counts."

"All racing shows is you're stronger and maybe faster. Winning at checkers shows I'm smarter."

-- -- --

"Come on, Mary. Let's race to the store and back."

"But it's ten blocks there and ten back."

"With our new roller skates we can do it in no time."

"Since we're only twelve we should ask our parents before we go far from home. My Father says I am not to go more than two blocks without first getting his permission."

"With our roller skates we can go ten blocks and back very quickly. Nobody but the two of us would ever know. I'm big for my age so nobody would dare bother us. Let's do it."

"If my Father ever found out I would be grounded for a month and probably forbidden to see you for a long time. I don't want that to happen. We have too much fun."

"Well I won't tell him if you don't. Besides there are a lot of people out and around in those ten blocks. I dare you to do it."

"You shouldn't dare me. It's not fair."

Suddenly she took off down the block skating as fast as she could. She was headed for the store. Caught by surprise,

Bill was behind by almost a half block before he could really get started.

"You tricked me just so you could get a big lead," he yelled.

"You taught me well," Mary yelled back. "I'm just using one of your tricks."

"I'll catch you before you get halfway to the store," was the reply Mary got.

At the store Mary still held about a ten foot lead. She did the turnaround much smoother than Bill and gained another ten feet. As Bill came out of his turn he hit a wider seam in the sidewalk and almost fell down. He caught himself and took off after Mary who had gained another ten feet.

Bill kept gaining slowly on Mary and after eight blocks coming back on the return leg he was dead even with her. Quickly Mary turned slightly in front of him causing him to swerve. This let her gain four or five feet and she made good use of it, hitting the finish line about six inches in the lead. She proceeded to heckle him about losing. Bill complained vigorously but knew, in the end, he probably would have done the same thing.

They decided to go in and see if they could talk Mary's Mother into giving them a piece of the cake she had baked that morning. As they started into the house Bill said, "Remember. Don't tell anyone about what we did."

Mary knew it was going to be difficult to not tell anybody she had won but she knew not telling was best for both of them.

-- -- --

"I love my new bicycle, Bill. The pink and white color is my favorite combination and it's very easy riding."

"I like my blue and white one also. The nice thing is we will never get them confused with each other. Plus, the blue and white is much better for a boy to have.

"Isn't it great being fourteen and having more freedom?"

"Yes. I'm really enjoying it. Would you like to have some fun?"

"You know I'm always up for some fun."

"Okay, let's have a bike race. We can go down the bike path starting just two blocks over. The lake in the park is three miles away. That would be a great distance to go. Six miles total should prove I'm faster than you are."

"Bill, there's only one way to prove it. You have to remember I won the race last week."

"You cheated. You cut me off at the second turn and besides the total distance was only three blocks."

"Three blocks is three blocks. It still proves something."

"OK, let's make sure we have an even and fair start. Let's line up at that seam in the sidewalk, and together count down from three to the start."

They moved forward to the seam and paused. Bill asked, "Ready?"

The answer from Mary was, "Yes, I am. Start the count."

Together they counted down, "three, two, one, GO." At GO they pushed off, slid into their seats, and started pedaling as fast as they could. At the two block point they turned, dead even, onto the bike path, still pedaling hard. Mary had been smart enough to pick the right side at the start which gave her the inside at the turn. Due to this she had about a two foot lead starting down the bike path. Neither of them realized just how long a three mile race was. By the time they got to the lake both were panting very heavily and skating slower.

37

Bill raised his hand and said, "Ten minute rest before we head back."

"OK," was the answer.

Ten minutes became twenty and then thirty as they rested, enjoying the view of the lake and enjoying just sitting and chatting. Finally, they looked at each other and Mary said, "How about we call it a tie and relax and try enjoying the ride back?"

"Sounds great. Let's rest here about ten minutes more before we start back?"

"I love the idea."

After ten minutes became fifteen they both got up, got on their bikes and pedaled back home, side by side and talking all the way. As they approached home both of them were realizing just how much they enjoyed the non-competitive ride back.

-- -- --

It was the biggest day of their lives. After strongly competing for so many years and then working together, and supporting each other for five years they realized just how good life could be together. The big day was their wedding day. They had spent several hours texting each other as they got ready to go to the church. The texts covered almost everything imaginable, ranging from "I love you" to guessing whose limousine would be at the church first. Obviously some of the old competitiveness still existed. The difference was now it's just another way to have fun and not the real competitive nature which existed for years.

Bill looked out the window towards the street and saw Mary's limousine pull up to the curb. That was when the competitive feeling bubbled up but it was quickly squelched as he realized Mary would need more time at the church to finish getting ready.

Besides, this way, she would be inside the church when he got there and thus not breach the old rule about not seeing the bride in her wedding dress before she started down the aisle. Bill went back to his bedroom to finish getting ready, and finally checked with his parents to see if they were ready to go. They were, so all three of them paraded out to their limousine and headed to the church.

Forty-five minutes later Bill was standing at the altar looking around amazed at how many people were in the church for the ceremony.

When the organist started playing the Wedding March, Bill looked up the aisle and saw Mary and her Father start down it. As Mary was about half way to the altar, the two of them looked at each other and realized just how much in love they were. They knew they were prepared for a long and happy marriage.

GREAT ENDINGS

As he rushed along, heading for his office, John Maxwell knew he had a very limited time to finish the plans on his new housing project. He also fully realized how important this was to his company. He had a meeting in three days with the building contractor and had to have the plans finalized and ready to go.

While crossing the street a colorful sign stapled to the telephone pole caught his eye. He quickly read it. It said, 'Lost, two dogs, both Lhasa apsos, Gone missing on Saturday. Reward for return.' It included pictures of both dogs and a number to call. Having no time to waste John quickly turned and proceeded on his way.

At his office, he kept thinking of the lost dogs. He knew they were small dogs and weren't as capable of protecting themselves as a larger dog, like a German Shepherd could. Nobody messed with a German Shepherd.

John sat down at his desk, pulled out the folders he needed and started working on the final plans for the developments. As he worked, his mind kept lingering on the lost dogs. He was reminded how much his two boys, Eric, five and Frank, seven, would love to have a dog. His wife, Marge, supported them in their wish, but was a little reluctant for fear that all of the work connected to having a dog could fall on her.

Finally, he pushed the lost dogs out of his mind and continued working until he felt he had a complete plan. He left messages for the Vice President and the Chief Financial Officer, asking them to check the plan over very carefully. He also reminded them he needed their final comments as soon as possible. Finally, as he headed back to his car, he stopped to read the posting in its entirety, noting the names of the dogs, Mickey and Moose, as well as the phone number of the owner. He didn't know why, but he had a feeling in the back of his mind he would need this information. John kept thinking of the dogs he had had as a youngster, and what losing them would have done to him.

Two days later, John met with his VP and CFO and they went over the complete details of the housing development. After a few small changes were made they declared the plan finished. They agreed there might be some other changes as construction went along, but for now, they were all happy and ready to get started.

Later, after his meeting with the contractor, John was at one of the construction sites where digging had started. One of the workmen said, "We got quite a surprise yesterday. There were two small dogs running through the site. I don't know where they came from, but one of our guys said he saw them yesterday as well. They must be running loose in the area."

This instantly piqued John's interest and he decided to stick around for a bit to see if the dogs came back. A couple of hours later no dogs had appeared, so John said to a workman, "If you see them again, try to catch them and call me. I can be here very quickly and I'll take them with me. I have the name and phone number of the owner.

Within a day John got a call and was informed the dogs had returned and were currently being held in one of the worker's vans. He was also told the dogs seemed friendly and harmless, but they were quite hungry. The workers had given the dogs meat out of their sandwiches. They had 'wolfed' it down and were seeking more.

"I'm on my way. I'll get some dog food before I get there," John said.

With that, John hung up and told his wife where he was going and what he was going to do. He told his family about the lost dogs and that they might be staying with them until the owners could be located.

His wife said, "Our boys are going to love that. They watch any dog shows on television and, as you know, they keep saying they would like to have a dog."

On the way to the construction site, John stopped at the pet store and bought a bag of dog food, two collars, and two leashes. At the site he was led to a Chevy van. He peeked in the side window and there were the dogs staring back at him. He opened the back door just enough to slide into the car. The dogs greeted him joyfully. He proceeded to put collars on them and attach the leashes. Finally, he opened the door wide, holding tightly onto the leashes. The Lhasas jumped out and tried to run over to the workers standing there with big grins on their faces.

John walked the dogs over to the workers, who moved towards them with a lot of petting of heads and backs. Finally John led the dogs to his car, opened a back door, and urged them to climb in. As they settled in, John started the car and headed for home with the dogs bouncing from window to window trying to see everything going past. At home John honked the horn as he pulled into the garage to alert everybody he was there.

When he opened the door into the house, his boys were bouncing up and down with great excitement. As the dogs came into the kitchen, the boys couldn't contain themselves. They hurried to the dogs as the dogs started wagging their tails and trying to get to them. Finally all four of them were bouncing up and down like they had known each other for years.

John unleashed the dogs and let all of them race through the house while he dug out soup bowls and poured dog food into them. At the sound of the dog food hitting the bowls, the dogs came charging back and dove in. John stood there watching and thinking, 'Maybe I should have bought two bags of food'. Their stomachs full, the dogs ran over to the boys with obvious intentions of staying with them.

John called the number he had copied from the poster. It rang five times followed by a recording saying, 'We're not home right now. Leave a short message and your phone number and we'll get back to you as soon as we can'.

John left a message saying he thought he had their missing dogs and that they were not harmed. He left his phone number and assumed he would get a reply later in the day.

Three days later, and still no response from the owners. John was starting to think the dogs might be his to keep. He knew, if that happened, his boys would really be happy.

Then, after a couple more days, John received a message from the owners of the dogs: "First, I have to apologize for the delay in returning your call. We had to go see my wife's family as her mother had gone into the hospital with heart problems. She seems to be doing all right for now. Second, we are tremendously happy our beloved dogs have been found. Our three kids are circling me here as gleeful as any kids ever were. Give me your address and we will be there as quick as we can. Again, thank you."

John quickly called them back and told them where he lived.

John watched from a window as a car pulled up in front of the house, and two adults and three kids hopped out and ran up on the porch. John had the door open for them, and as they came in, the kids were calling 'Mickey, Moose'. John could hear the dogs barking as they hurried from the den to the front door. The three kids sat down on the floor, and the dogs climbed all over them, barking constantly.

As all of the furor was going on, the man introduced himself as Bill Cassell and his wife Joan and pointed to their kids saying, "That is George, Mary and Ronald. The dogs got out when someone didn't lock the gate on the fence. I'd like to give you the reward for finding our precious animals."

John replied, "Why don't you give the money to charity instead."

"That would be fine with me." Bill smiled as he rounded up his dogs and to take them all home.

John said, "The dogs were really filthy. We gave them a bath and they didn't object too much." "Thanks. We really appreciate that," Bill said as he and his wife took their group out to the car.

After they were all gone, John and Marge tried to settle down to their normal life, but everyone felt the loss of the dogs. This was particularly true for the two boys, who were really unhappy. After only a week at their home they felt like part of the family.

Three days later when John came home from work he was carrying a Yorkie puppy. The boys heard the yipping and came running.

"You found another dog", proclaimed Eric. "Do you know who the owner is?"

"Yes, I do. You and Frank are the owners. I brought him home for you."

The gleeful looks in their eyes were worth a million dollars. The boys immediately started playing with the puppy.

That evening, as John and Marge were enjoying television while listening to all the yells and barking coming from the den, John commented, "You really get used to having them around, don't you?"

Marge said, "Do you mean the kids or the dogs?"

"Both, actually."

THE GOLDEN YEARS

Heading for the entrance of the Golden Nugget restaurant, John Pastor was hoping there wasn't a long line. Quite often the line extended out the door. When that happened he would turn around and head elsewhere. The fact there were parking spaces available was usually a good indicator the line was manageable. Entering the restaurant, he saw there were only ten people in line to get seated. He knew the Golden Nugget would seat all of them quickly.

As John joined the line, the first four people were called for seating. "*Great,*" John said to himself. "*Now there's only six people ahead of me.*" His thoughts were lingering on his wife, whom he had lost to cancer two years before. He stood there contemplating his life as a fifty-eight year old widower starting to wonder where his life was going. He was starting to think about trying to date again, as well as getting into going to the casino for a little gambling fun. His wife never wanted him to do this.

Minutes later the hostess had seated the six people in front of him and when she came back she asked, "How many?" John indicated he was alone so she led him to a small table. He picked up the menu and looked through it to decide what he wanted. After making his decision, he sat back and looked around at the other diners. He noticed an attractive lady two tables to his left who appeared to be about his age. She was obviously trying to decide about lunch since she went from page to page and back again in the menu.

Just then the waitress came to the lady's table and, "Hi, Betty. Glad to see you again. Do you want your usual?"

Betty said, "No. I'm going to get something different today." She gave the waitress her order. Then the waitress came over to John's table and asked him the same thing. He replied he had, and proceeded to give her his order. As he settled back in his chair to relax, wait, and start on his cup of coffee, he looked over and the lady was doing exactly the same thing. *'Hmmm,'* thought John, *'I see she knows how to lean back and relax also. She looks like she would be someone interesting to know.'*

Ten minutes later the waitress came back with both John's and Betty's food. As they dug in, the waitress refilled their coffee cups.

John finished eating and signaled for the waitress to bring his bill. The waitress asked if everything had been all right. John said, "Yes, it always is." The waitress said she would bring him his bill.

Betty spoke up, saying, "I need my bill too. Everything tasted great as usual."

The waitress responded, "OK, I'll bring your bill right away."

The waitress quickly returned with the bills and gave them to Betty and John. The two of them started digging for money. John laid his money on top of his bill and the proper tip beside his plate.

Meanwhile Betty continued looking through her purse and making low muttering noises. Walking by, John heard her comment, "I don't believe it. I'm two dollars short of meeting my bill and tip. I can't just short tip her. I'm here too often to get the reputation of a bad tipper."

When the waitress came back to take the money, Betty told her she didn't know what to do. "I am short two dollars of having enough money to meet the tip and the bill." The waitress knew Betty ate there often and offered to let her pay the next time she was in. Betty was reluctant to do that since she is not sure when she would return. It could be a matter of weeks.

John said," I couldn't help overhearing. I'm John Pastor and I could give you the two dollars if it would help."

As the waitress started to smile Betty replied, "I'm Betty Dunwell and I need to say no to your offer. Did you say you were Pastor John? What church are you with?"

"No. It's John Pastor, not Pastor John. I do go to church, but I'm not ordained."

They talked for a couple of minutes and in the end she accepted the two dollars with the proviso he give her his phone number so she could be sure to refund his money.

He replied, "Well, let's trade phone numbers. That way either of us can get in touch with the other about the two dollars."

She agreed.

They left the restaurant together trying to find something to talk about. It turned out they were parked next to each other. She got out her keys, pressed the unlock button and nothing happened. The battery in the key fob was dead. She fumbled around trying to get the key in the keyhole. He offered to help her with it.

She commented, "I haven't had to open a car door with the key for a few years now."

He unlocked the door, and they stood talking to each other. They discovered they were born two miles apart in

Piqua, Ohio and they both enjoy the philharmonic orchestra, plays at the local theaters, and martinis.

During this discussion she told John she had been a widow for five years. Her husband was killed in a car wreck by a drunk driver. John offered his consolation and told her about his wife's cancer death. They got into a discussion of hobbies they enjoyed, which included reading, games on the computer, walking, and travelling.

They then planned to meet at the Golden Nugget in a couple of weeks, with both secretly looking forward to another meeting. They decided on a date and time to meet again.

At the get together, they chatted constantly throughout their meal and talked for twenty-five minutes after they finished. Every time their favorite waitress passed the table she just grinned and kept moving.

John and Betty met at the restaurant every two weeks for a while and then started meeting there every week. John started picking Betty up at her place and they went to the Golden Nugget every other day.

The waitress' grin got bigger and bigger as she stopped at the table and said, "I assume I'm invited to the wedding."

Betty quickly said, "Yes, of course you are invited. It's going to be the eighteenth of next month at five pm. I brought you this card. It has the address of the church where the ceremony will be held."

The waitress replied, "I'll plan on being there. Thank you. Where are you going on your honeymoon?"

"Right after the wedding we're catching a plane to Bermuda and plan to spend two weeks in the sunshine, really learning about each other."

"That sounds great. I wish I could go."

"Well, we're not going to invite you to join us."

THE REUNION

As Jessie walked into the restaurant to get a bite to eat for lunch she heard someone call her name.

"Jessie? Is that really you? I haven't seen you since we retired twelve years ago."

Harry thought, *'It's amazing. She's still a true blonde with no fading or graying evident.'*

She turned towards the voice, recognizing the face. "Harry? Has it been that long ago? It seems like only a few years. It's really good to see you again."

'He's still elegant looking and carries himself so well. There are slight signs of graying but his still bright green eyes don't really let you notice that', Jessie was thinking.

"You don't look a day older than you did when we retired twelve years ago, but, I think it seems like only a few years because we both were so glad to retire from the company.

"Well, you certainly don't look like twelve years has passed. Maybe only two or three.

"How have you been doing in retirement besides staying young looking and pretty?".

Jessie looked away for a moment before looking back. "Until six months ago everything was great. John and I were involved in many things and doing quite a bit of traveling. Then they found cancer in John's liver. Testing showed it had spread to several of his other organs. We've been in and out of numerous hospitals while they treated this."

"I'm sorry to hear about his troubles. Retirement is supposed to be a great time of life, but those kinds of problems seem to always be occurring. Can I do anything to help?"

"Not at this point. It's just a matter of waiting and seeing what happens. How are you and Harriet doing?"

It was Harry's turn to look down for a second and then back. "After I retired we got involved in a lot of things like you and John. Traveling was our big thing, but not to conferences."

Jessie laughed out loud, "That's the first time in a while I have had a good belly laugh. Thank you, I needed it. How is Harriet doing?"

"That's my cross to bear. She died in an automobile accident three years ago. A drunken driver texting, ran a red light. Harriet was killed instantly. I still miss her terribly. I hardly know what to do with myself."

Jessie stopped smiling. "Harry, you don't know how sad that makes me feel. I sympathize with you.

"Jessie, if you haven't eaten yet why don't you join me here and we can talk about everything. After all, we have twelve years to catch up on."

"Thank you, I think I will," Jessie said as she pulled out a chair and sat down.

"Which hospital is your husband in and what is happening with him?"

"He's in Memorial Hospital right now. He's heavily sedated to get him ready for more surgery tomorrow morning."

Harry frowned, "You have all of my sympathy for what you're going through. Despite the shock it's sort of a blessing my wife didn't linger and suffer before passing away."

Jessie's eyes teared up and Harry quickly apologized for saying what he had in light of the problems her husband had.

Jessie held up her hand, "You don't need to apologize. I understand your feelings completely. Why don't we give our orders to the waitress?"

Harry signaled for the waitress, they placed their lunch orders, and continued their discussion of where they used to work with Jessie saying, "In reality, you were one of the few upper level people I really enjoyed working with over the years I spent there."

While they were talking Harry was thinking, *'Jessica still looks as lovely as the day we worked together. She was always under-appreciated at work. She did a great job, but was always very quiet while doing it. I may have been the only one who truly appreciated what she did and how well she did it.'*

The only good thing either of them had to say about the place was they both had stayed long enough to be able to draw a reasonable retirement pay. Neither of them mentioned their respective spouses for the rest of the lunch. After they had eaten and exchanged cell phone numbers each went their own way. Jessie headed back to the hospital to spend the evening near her sedated husband while Harry headed home to finish some cleaning he had started the day before.

The next day the writing group to which Harry belonged got together over lunch to discuss the new anthology they were putting together. They had chosen the topic "The Best and Worst of Life". Harry was working on a story about both ends of the topic. His group had a goal of getting the anthology published before the end of the year so they had six months to finish their stories and pull everything together. As each of the ten members of the group talked about what they were writing, Harry's mind kept returning to Jessie's husband and his surgery. He decided he would try calling her later in the afternoon. Most surgeries were scheduled for early morning, by late afternoon they would have a good idea of the results.

After the writing group broke up, Harry went home to watch the NBA basketball game to relax. He went to sleep in his easy chair, finally waking up at five pm. He fixed himself a glass of iced tea and got his cell phone from the dresser. He proceeded to call Jessie's number.

After four rings she answered, "Hello Harry. How was your day?"

"My day was fine. My writing group met and I got some things done I needed to do. More importantly, how was your day. How is John? How did the surgery go? Is John OK?"

"Things went better than expected. John is still sedated. They're bringing him out of it slowly while they keep a close eye on everything. It looks good at this point."

"That's great. I'm rooting for both of you. I'll check back tomorrow. Right now I'll put on my pj's and watch a movie I recorded the other night."

"What movie?", Jessie asked.

"It's 'Alice In Wonderland', made in 1933 and stars Gary Cooper, W. C. Fields, Cary Grant, and Charlotte Henry. They made a lot of really good classic movies in the thirties without all of the computer animation they use now. I'm really looking forward to watching it."

"Sounds like an interesting movie," Jessie replied. "I've always enjoyed watching a Cary Grant movie. He was such a great actor and handsome too."

Harry smiled, "Well, a handsome actor means more to you than it would to me. Now an actress like Marilyn Monroe is a different matter. Beautiful beyond belief. I have the movie on DVR if you would like to see it sometime?"

"I need to get back to the hospital and check on John. Maybe we could do lunch again soon."

"Anytime. Just give me a call. Maybe John can join us in the near future.."

"That would be really nice. Goodbye for now."

Harry said a quick goodbye as Jessie hung up. He decided to get a cold beer, fix himself a snack, and watch his movie. When he woke up he realized he had slept through the last third of the movie. He backed up to where he remembered what happened and finished watching the movie. He proceeded to put on his pajamas and to jump into bed to watch the evening news. Suddenly the phone rang.

When he picked up the phone the first thing he heard was sobbing and a mumbled voice saying something. He waited a few seconds

"Jessie? Is that you? What's wrong?"

"Oh, Harry, John has taken a turn for the worse. The doctors are with him now trying to find out what happened. They think his system may have been too weak for the surgery. They say he is critical at this point and could go either way."

"Is there anything I can do?"

"The doctor said I can only wait and see. I'll call if anything changes," Jessie replied between sobs.

As Harry hung up the phone he decided he needed another beer and headed toward the fridge. After finishing the beer, he realized how tired he was so he hopped into bed, turned out the light, and was asleep in ten minutes.

The next morning when he woke his thoughts returned to all of the events of the previous evening. The more he thought about them the more helpless he felt at not being able to do anything to help Jessie. He knew the doctor was right in saying all Jessie could do was wait and see.

Harry spent the day trying to finish some projects around the house he had started a few days before. It helped take his mind off Jessie and John. As evening approached he decided to call Jessie. The phone rang four times and Harry started to wonder and worry about what might be going on. Finally after six rings Jessie answered the phone.

"Jessie, this is Harry. Have there been any changes? What's going on?"

"There have been no changes as of yet. John's sedated and being watched carefully by the doctors."

"Have you had any supper? Do you have any plans for it?"

"I haven't given it any thought. I'm planning on being here at the hospital for most of this evening."

"Why don't you let me take you some place for supper. I know several good restaurants near the hospital. I suspect you need the break."

"Yes. Thank you for the offer, I accept. What time did you have in mind?"

"How about six? I'll pick you up at the entrance to the hospital and return you there after we eat."

"Sounds good.

"OK. See you at six."

Harry arrived at the entrance to the hospital promptly at six and found Jessie waiting for him. As she got into the car he asked, "How is John doing?"

"There hasn't really been a change," she responded. "He seems to be holding his own for now."

"Well, that's good news."

"That's what I keep telling myself. Where are we going to eat?," Jessie asked.

"There's a good seafood place about three miles down the road. By the way dinner is on me. Don't give me any argument."

About ten minutes later, Harry pulled into the parking lot at a restaurant called 'Perfect Seafood' and rolled into a parking space. As they entered the place, the hostess greeted them, took them to a table, and gave them menus. "Anthony will be here shortly to take your orders. Our special tonight is baked cod fresh from the ocean. Enjoy your meals."

Both Jessie and Harry ordered the cod. As they waited for their food to come they continued talking about their working days. As they ate they continued talking about their working days. After they finished eating they continued talking about their working days.

Finally Jessie commented, "I have to get back to the hospital to check on John. I really want to thank you for this break. I really needed it. With any luck John will have shown some improvement when I get back."

"I hope so. I'm glad I could be of some help. If you need anything please give me a call."

As Harry headed home, he knew he had really enjoyed the evening. He waited a few days, then contacted Jessie again to talk about a thought which had occurred to him. He suggested as long as John was in the hospital the two of them should get together for lunch once a week. It would help the pain both of them were feeling. They could talk about their respective spouses, the good things, the fun things, even the difficulties.

Jessie answered, "I agree it is a good idea. I'm so glad we met up again. Knowing you're here for me helps me feel less alone. That's something I haven't felt in a long time."

Harry said, "I'm glad I could be there to help. I do understand what you are going through."

For the next three months Harry and Jessie got together once a week for lunch, their occasional phone calls becoming more frequent. Harry was starting to feel less pain over the loss of his wife and Jessie had a friendly ear to talk to about John and his problems as well as the changes from week to week. During this period John oscillated up and down, sometimes showing significant improvement followed by a descent back to an extremely poor condition.

At the end of three months when Harry called to go to lunch he realized Jessie was crying uncontrollably and could hardly talk. He immediately realized what had happened. John's problems had finally won out.

Jessie was finally able to tell Harry that John had passed away overnight. She had started the process of finalizing funeral arrangements as well as everything else involved in settling the affairs of his estate.

Three weeks later when they got together for lunch Harry said, "You shouldn't be by yourself at this time. You need to get out and do things. You need something to occupy your mind. My writing group is meeting three days from now. I remember years back you were working on a novel. Why don't you join us You can just listen at first if you want. Writing a novel is a process requiring a lot of thought and attention and as such should help take your mind off everything that has happened."

Jessie asked, "Are you writing a novel?"

"No, I just write short stories. I think they can be more fun than writing a novel and it doesn't take as long to produce something worth bragging about."

"I think I will join you for the meeting. It sounds like a very interesting group."

Were they eventually married? Certainly. They lived happily ever after.

THE PEDICURE

"**B**ut Helen, I've never had that done before."

With a smile Helen said, "Oh shut up Bill. Put your shoes on and let's get this over with."

Slowly he put his shoes on, all the time mumbling under his breath.

"What are you mumbling about? Either speak up or be quiet. You're going to get this pedicure regardless of what you say or do."

"It'll probably hurt me. They might accidentally cut a to off. I'll stay home."

"The devil you say. Get in the car, with or without your shoes. You have been complaining about having trouble cutting your toenails for six months now and, no matter what you think or say, we are going to get this done. Do you understand me?"

"Yes, Yes, I understand you, but I didn't think I was complaining that much and I still don't want to go."

"Your prime complaints are, at your age, you can't stay bent over long enough to cut all ten toenails. You've, also, been complaining that with your bifocals things never quite come into good enough focus and you're afraid you'll cut yourself with the clippers, so I'm not giving you a choice."

"You promise not to tell any of the guys about this. I couldn't stand their kidding and they'll get really mean about it. I know those guys."

"I promise I'll only tell the ladies in my bridge group," Helen said with a great big smile on her face.

"You've got to be kidding," Bill responded. "They are the wives of seven of my best friends."

"I won't tell anybody. Ok?"

"You're still grinning at me. I'm not sure you mean it."

"I swear on a stack of hundred dollar bills I won't tell anybody"

"Now I know you really mean it."

"I made an appointment for each of us," said Helen, trying very hard to suppress another big grin.

Bill finally put on his socks and shoes, got out of his chair, and started towards the garage. Halfway there he quietly said to himself, "I think I can still make a break for it if I run fast enough."

"I heard you. You try it and I'll get in the car and chase you down, and you know that won't take very far. Get in the car. I'll drive."

"You realize you owe me big time for this."

"I think you are going to be so happy you'll offer to buy me dinner at my favorite restaurant."

"Well Helen, I might do that anyway, just because you are trying to be so nice to me. I love you, you know."

"I know, and it is reciprocated. We will be at the pedicure shop in about ten minutes. Your appointment is first, so we can talk about dinner on the way home."

Shortly they pulled into the Mall parking lot and approached 'Nails and Toes' shop.

Bill again started to have regrets over all of this, but decided he was too committed to not go into the shop. As they checked in, Bill saw the price breakout listing 'Pedicures forty-eight dollars'.

"Look at that price. I could buy something I want with that money."

Helen answered, "Well, just imagine what you could buy when you add the tip to that amount."

At that point a young lady walked up to them and said, "Hi, my name is Marie. Who's first?"

Helen pointed at Bill and said, "Take him. This is his first time and he needs to get started."

As Bill followed Marie to one of the plush looking chairs he was thinking, Well, this part is not too bad. She's good looking. But she's, obviously, at least forty years younger than I am, so I better concentrate on the pedicure.

As he sat down Marie reached over and turned on the back massager mechanism. A few seconds later He commented," This part really feels good. I hope the rest is the same."

After Marie helped him off with his shoes and socks, she asked him to put his feet in the warm water foot bath. Bill's thought was, Nice.

Marie worked her way through the whole process: wash the feet, clip the nails and cuticals, feet back in water to soak a bit, then out again, moisturizer, dry thoroughly. Finally Bill was told to put on his socks and shoes, he was done.

Helen, sitting in the chair next to him getting her toenails painted said to Marie, "Ask him if he would like his toenails painted pink."

Marie looked up at him and said, "We have several nice shades of pink you can choose from. I can show them to you."

Bill sank a little lower in his chair saying, "I'll make you a deal Helen. I'll let her paint one little toe if you will buy me a new laptop computer I want. I can always wear socks with my new sandals."

"Nobody wears socks with sandals. A pedicure and toenail paint is what makes your feet look so good while wearing sandals," Helen answered.

Just then Bill looked out the front window and saw their next door neighbor walking past. The neighbor looked in the window, moved closer, and waved hello to Bill and Helen. Bill grabbed a magazine and held it in front of his face. As he peeked around the magazine, he saw the neighbor open the front door and say, "Hi Bill. Are you done yet, or are you getting a permanent also?" The grin on the guys face said he was completely enjoying all of this as he started to leave.

Bill turned towards the back wall, sank even lower in his chair, and said, "Oh my God, he's going to tell all of the neighbors and the guys in our poker club. I'll never live this down."

"Oh don't worry. They'll all forget about this in a few years. At least by ten years from now."

Bill could tell Helen was just about to burst as she struggled to keep from laughing.

Finally Helen said, "If you'll finish putting on your socks and shoes, I'll pay the bill and we can go get dinner. Ok?"

A few minutes later as they approached their car, Bill turned to Helen. "Since the pedicure felt so good, I'm going to take you to 'The Sea Loft' and buy you a good seafood dinner. But I warn you, I'll never get a pedicure without you along. How often can we go?"

After dinner they headed home. As they pulled into their driveway they saw six of the neighbors standing beside the house next door. All six neighbors gathered around the car Bill and Helen were in, and started making joking comments, such as, "Show us your toes", "Did you get a permanent?",

"Did you pick out a color for your toenails?" "Are you going shopping for a dress tomorrow? I know where you can get a nice facial".

Bill quickly pulled into the garage and punched the button to close the garage door. He could still hear the neighbors yelling comments as they went into the house. Bill's only comment was, "I think I'll stay in the house for the week and only go out at night."

Helen answered, "Sleep on it and go out and face them tomorrow. They'll quit pretty quickly if you ignore them."

"You're sure of that?"

"Yes. I know them quite well."

BAD IN BUSINESS

F red Puller was wondering why he had to come all
the way downtown to recover the money he had
paid for a set of pricey mail order ballpoint pens which,
it turned out, were defective. It almost wasn't worth the
trouble and he had seriously considered just forgetting about
it. After all it was only thirty dollars. He finally decided
he couldn't let the company get away with selling a faulty
product. It was the principle of the thing.

As he was walking out of the parking lot, he was totaling
up how much it was costing him to get his thirty dollars back.
Ten dollars for parking, cost of gas, plus the time he was
spending. It started to seem like a stupid thing to do, but, alas,
he was here now so he continued. It was a five block walk
to the company where he was headed. He was getting a little
bit of exercise for the effort. Exercise may be the only thing
he would get out of it, but its still the principle of the thing.

Riding the elevator up to the sixth floor of the Brandor
Building he was trying to compose how he would handle
this. He could play it politely and see if they would cooperate
about returning his money, or he could go in fighting mode
and just attack the customer service person.

"Bing". The elevator doors presented him to the office
straight ahead. The sign above the door read, 'Executive

Offices, Brandor Manufacturing'. Fred walked over to the door and gently pushed it open. There was no one at the receptionist's desk. Fred thought that was a little strange, but then he saw a sign saying, 'Out to Lunch, Back in One Hour'. He didn't know if he should leave or just take a seat and wait. He decided the choice was obvious. If he left he would probably never come back and he would have to resort to e-mail or telephone to accomplish his mission, and it would be just too easy for them to hit 'Delete' or hang up. Also, Fred preferred people contact versus automated service.

Hearing soft voices from an inner office, Fred walked over to the door. As he approached it, the voices became more and more audible. Standing about a foot and a half from the door he could clearly hear two men speaking.

First voice: "John, did you get to the meeting with Stanson Industries?"

Second voice: "Yes sir, I did. I'm working on the results of that meeting. About another half-hour, and I'll have it ready for you."

"Go ahead and tell me the basics of what went on."

"As you know, they are in some of the same areas of manufacturing that we are. There was lengthy discussion of procedures to optimize profits."

"Well, Steve, everyone felt the best way to accomplish this was to minimize variations in prices. This could be done by control of the actual profit margin. They agreed with both of our companies that setting the profit to be maintained was the best way to keep control. If we compete against each other and let the profit margins float, we would tend to minimize income for both companies. The second big item discussed was how best to keep taxes on income low. Everyone felt that the best way to do this was to maintain an off-shore account and deposit a set amount of money in it each month. Everyone agreed on the set amount of twenty-five percent. This will definitely reduce our taxes and it is almost impossible to detect."

"Well John, I think this will work into a very good plan and will maximize our company's income. Get the full report to me as soon as you can. When I have it I will consult the Chief Executive Officer of Stanson Industries and try to get all of the little details in place. He and I will have to work closely on this to maintain secrecy."

"You did a good piece of work, John. I think I can see a great Christmas bonus coming up for you. In fact, as CEO of Brandor Manufacturing, I can guarantee it."

"Thank you, sir. As a matter of fact, my wife and I are planning on spending the New Year's Eve holiday in Hawaii and, that will certainly come in handy."

"Sounds great. Enjoy it."

Fred crept slowly to the entry door and left. His next thought was what should he do with what he overheard.

As Fred went out the door, he looked at the sign for Brandor Manufacturing and saw it said 'CEO-Steve Battles, CFO-John Harshmore. He wrote those names and positions down for future reference.

Fred's thoughts as he headed to his car was, "What the devil is going on here? These guys are apparently cheating the public and the IRS. The problem is, I can never prove it. Not really. It would just be my word against theirs. They, almost obviously, have a set of cooked books to show the authorities. I think I need to go home and think about this. But, first, I really need something to eat and, I need a good martini right now. I'm glad nobody knows I was in their outer office.

Later in the evening, Fred was sitting in his living room trying to decide what to do. He felt his best option was just to shut up and mind his own business, which was really what he was inclined to do. Perhaps watching TV for a few hours would help take his mind off the whole thing.

When he woke up three hours later, he felt fuzzy headed. It took him a bit to come fully awake, and recall everything that had happened. He remembered he had to do something. The real question was what.

Fred's first thought was to contact the local police department, but he realized that was a little too close to home and might increase the chances of repercussions from the crooked people. He thought a good choice would be the FBI. He finally decided that a State organization would be the best choice, but which one? The State Police, a State Congressional Committee, or some other State office? He knew he needed to do some research, so he googled 'State Offices' for the State of Ohio and started going through all of the listings available.

As he searched through the listing of offices and bureaus, Fred quickly realized that the Attorney General's office might be the best place to contact and maybe the safest place to send his information. If they accepted it and started checking on the companies, they would also bring the FBI into it because of cheating on Federal taxes.

That evening Fred typed up all he had heard and knew about the two companies, Brandor Manufacturing and Stanson Industries. Then he started on a package to mail to the Attorney General's office. He felt his biggest problem would be how to stay anonymous. He very much wanted to keep his name out of it. He decided to sleep on his decision.

The next day he continued as originally planned. He knew his only real action was to put the package of information together and mail it to the Attorney General's office. Fred knew an anonymous package of information was not enough, but presently it was all he had and he needed to get it in the mail, hoping it would, at the least, arouse enough interest to get some official follow-up.

"I've got everything ready to mail. I'll run over to the post office and get it on its way. Then I can wait and see what happens."

When the package arrived at the Attorney General's office, the secretary dropped it, unopened, on the desk of one of the lawyers working there. The lawyer looked at it, front and back, noting there was no return address. He started to toss it in the wastebasket. As he turned in his chair, he said quietly to himself, "I'd better, at least, see what it is." He opened it, pulled out the contents, again noting no return address, and no signature. Then he started to read it. He read through everything in the package, jumped up, went into the Attorney General's office to talk to him about it. After reviewing everything the AG decided they needed to pursue it far enough to find out if the facts supported the allegations.

After two weeks of checking out everything they could, the AG made it a top item for their office to follow up. At this point he had indications of what was going on but no solid proof yet.

After conferring with the Governor, the AG decided to make a public announcement about the case to see what could be stirred up. "I have called this press conference to announce we are looking into possible illegal actions by several local companies. I will not identify them at this point, nor will I identify how this information was received. We hope to have more information in the near future and we will make a more detailed announcement at that time."

After the press conference the AG had a second meeting with the Governor, and informed him they still did not know for sure who had provided the information, but they had a few clues.

A week and a half later the AG went into the Governor's office with a great big smile on his face. "We have a witness who has evidence of what has been going on. This person is a secretary and office manager for one of the companies involved in all of this. She said she decided the best thing for her to do is be completely honest, even though it might get her in trouble with the law as well. I indicated to her that for complete information on the matter, we would provide immunity for her. She, then, gave us letters, emails, recorded phone calls, all of which totally verify what we were told was going on. It also proves there was a third company involved in this corruption."

"Great. Let's move on it," said the AG.

With the information the office manager, Linda Johnson, provided, the case against all three companies was a cinch. The judge showed no mercy for the companies.

After the judge stopped smiling, he found them guilty as charged and fined them each five million dollars, resulting in a total loss of seventy-five million dollars in State and Federal funding.

During the trial the names of both Fred Puller and the Office Manager, a twenty-five year old lady named Patricia Patterson, were revealed.

Three weeks later Fred was sitting in a restaurant waiting for his food to be served, when he saw Patricia Patterson come in the front door. He caught her attention and commented, "It's nice to see you again, Patricia."

"Hello, Doctor Puller. After all we've been through, you can call me Pat," she responded.

"Well then, you should call me Fred. We do have a lot in common. Why don't you join me?"

"Thank you. I think I will."

BAD IN CLASS

As soon as Dr. Fred Puller entered the room he knew something was going on with some of the students. He had taught at Phillip Johnson High School for fifteen years, long enough to be able to recognize problems.

He looked around the room full of students, trying to make a mental judgment about each of them. For a new class this is usually difficult to do, but there were, always, some students for whom it was easy. It appeared to him a group of two boys and three girls in the back row would fall into this category easily. Fred knew this was the first year at Johnson High for those five students and as far as he knew there had been no problems with them previously.

He walked over to his desk in the front of the room, and noticed those five leaning over, whispering to each other and trying to keep from laughing out loud. When he reached the desk he turned to address the class. As he called roll he noted the names of the five: Robert, Harry, Josie, Mary, and Becky.

"Good morning all. I'm Dr. Puller and this is the class on General Science with an emphasis on physics."

At the mention of 'physics' the group in the back row let out a burst of laughter and quickly clapped their hands over their mouths.

"I understand that 'physics' can have more than one meaning, but none of them are funny. Now if all of you will pull out your notebooks, we'll start with a short outline of the class and get into the basics of physics.

The mention of physics again caused the five to snicker loudly behind their hands. Fred gave them a harsh look. "Would you like to spend the rest of the hour in the principal's office?"

With that they settled down and tried to start paying attention. As Fred talked they continued looking around, obviously not really paying attention. At least they were being quiet.

The bell ending the class sounded. Fred asked the group to stay and talk to him. He started out by asking why they felt they could interrupt class like they did. They hemmed and hawed a bit before Robert spoke.

"We really feel we are the elite in this school and this gives us more freedom to do what we please."

The astonished Fred couldn't believe his ears. "You really think you have more power in this class than I do? That may be the most preposterous thing I've ever heard. I have the power to take you to the principal's office or to banish you from my class. What do you have to say?"

Again the hesitating started and continued for a longer time while the five continued looking back and forth at each other. Finally Mary spoke, "Well yes, you do have the power to do all of that, but we were told you weren't as forceful as some of the other teachers. We thought we would push you to try to find your limits. I think we found them."

"Actually you exceeded them by quite a lot. If you give me any more problems all of you will go immediately to the principal's office. Do you understand?"

"Yes sir, we understand completely. We'll not disturb your class again," Josie, another girl in the group, said.

Fred made a mental note that Robert had really said the most and he wondered why.

As the students left for their next class, Fred headed for the principal's office to talk to him about what had happened. Fred related the events that had occurred and the principal made the point this group was known to be involved in other things, cruelly teasing other kids being a prime one. There was also some suspicion they were involved with marijuana.

This information told Fred these five kids needed some strong leadership to steer them in the right direction. He volunteered to take the lead in trying to change their attitudes and beliefs. "I think I know a couple of people who could be of help in achieving it." Fred and the principal discussed various ways to go about doing it. The principal then called the Education Board, explained what was going on and what needed to be done. The Board finally gave their approval to go ahead. With that decision the principal gave Fred full approval to get started. He requested Fred report to him regularly. They decided once a week for the first three months would be best, and after that monthly.

At the first weekly meeting, Fred talked to the kids about the things being said about them. When bullying was mentioned they just giggled lightly. At the mention of marijuana they giggled again, but managed to stifle it. The three girls glanced at each other, then looked down as though they might feel some shame. The two boys just gave Fred a look implying, 'you can't prove it, so don't even mention it to us'.

It became obvious all had egos exceeding their capabilities of understanding the potential consequences of what they were doing. Fred knew he needed some way of getting them to understand the reality of what they were doing and the probable, very bad, results.

At the second meeting, Fred brought in Dr. Paul Davidson from the local University, an Ethics and Human Resources instructor and Dr. John Haverstick, a well-known medical doctor so they could talk about the interaction of science and life and how the two could lead to a fuller, more useful existence. The three of them talked about achieving a much more useful and satisfying life. This was intended to be a lead-in to what one could accomplish in life without criminal actions. The girls seemed to be generally in agreement, but the boys just sat back and didn't say anything, although they did appear to nod a few times.

Fred knew he had a difficult job ahead of him. He needed to take a major step in his efforts to help the group. At the end of the school day he went to the principal's office and they further discussed Fred's plan. The principal listened to the details of the plan again. His final words were, "If that doesn't resolve this whole thing, there's probably no hope for them. Proceed with my complete approval."

At the end of class the next day, Fred sat down with the five and told them of friends of his who got involved with drugs in college and were now either in jail, living on the streets with a police record, or dead.

Two of the girls, Josie and Becky, along with Harry seemed to understand what was being pointed out to them. By their inattention, it was obvious the other two boys wasn't fully appreciative of what was said. Fred made the point that his former friends were smart enough to get in college and achieve high grades, but then drug use destroyed their lives. He also noted all five of them were going in the same direction his friends had because they were letting drugs control them.

"What do each of you want to do in your lives, both near and far? Do you have any plans at all?"

Robert immediately responded, "I think I'm smart enough to not let drugs control me."

Fred's response was, "So did my friends, but drug use got complete control of them."

Mary spoke, "Are you just making this up to scare us? Can you prove the stuff about your former friends or are you just lying to us?"

Fred replied, "I hadn't planned on doing this but all of you are coming downtown and I'll introduce you to some of my friends from college, if I can find the alley they now occupy. Friday, after school, we'll make a trip. All of you can tell your parents you'll be going on a special project and that you need a signed permission slip. Also that you'll be home about an hour later than usual. OK?"

They all agreed to take the jaunt. Their curiosity was increasing.

On Friday, after the bell rang, all of them went out to the parking lot and climbed into Fred's van. Fifteen minutes later they were parked downtown. After leaving the van, they all followed Fred as he walked along, peering into alleys as they went. Finally Fred stopped, turned into an alley, and walked into it, towards three people huddled against a row of trash cans. All three of them were ragged and appeared not to have bathed for a very long time.

"Hi guys. How's it going? Have you had anything to eat yet today?"

They all shook their heads back and forth. One responded, "Hi Fred. Did you bring us supper so we don't have to search all of the garbage cans for something edible? You can get us some carry-out at the pizza place across the street."

"I can get you some, but first I want you to meet some students of mine. They didn't believe me when I told them I knew all of you."

Fred turned to his students, "These guys have several college degrees between them. Why don't you talk to them while I go get some pizzas."

Fred headed across the street while the students tentatively approached the men. All of them looked like they hadn't shaved or had a haircut in months.

"Do you guys really have all those college degrees?," Robert asked.

All of the guys told what degrees they had. They included two Bachelors of Science, one Bachelor of Arts, one Masters of Art, and one Masters of History. The student's eyes kept growing wider as the homeless men talked. The three men started telling what had happened to them.

One told about his starting to dabble with drugs as a freshman in college. Several of his friends encouraged him to do so, plus he found out the girls he met who were doing drugs provided easy sex. The drugs finally came to control his life.

Another said he didn't get involved in drugs until his senior year in college, but as he continued in the Master's degree program his usage increased greatly. He managed to get his degree, but found he was too far into drugs to stop and they controlled his life. That's how he got where he was today.

Finally the last one said he had started in high school with a group of so-called friends. He had managed to keep it under reasonable control, getting totally stoned only about once a month. He carried that pattern through college, but in trying for his Master's degree, he got deeper and deeper into the drugs. When his mentor found he had offered drugs to a couple of other students who were helping him on his thesis, he was told to leave and to never come back.

Finally Fred arrived with three large pizzas and gave each of the shabby men one.

Becky asked the men if they had been friends with Fred in college. All three acknowledged Fred had been a friend of theirs and had tried very hard to get them off of drugs. They all said they had ignored Fred, and he had eventually gone his own way towards his Doctorate. They also emphasized if they had listened to Fred they would never have gotten to where they were now. They dove into their pizzas as Fred led his students back to the van. As they walked, Fred asked them if what they had heard and seen was the future they wanted. All five were silent until they got near the van and then the girls started to cry. The two boys looked like they were on the verge of tears too.

"I never thought it could get to anything as bad as that," Robert said." It would be a terrible life, and I don't want anything to do with it. We're only doing drugs once in a while, but then we got into the teasing because we thought it was funny. We should have never done either one."

The girls cried harder. "I'll tell you everything you want to know, including where we got the drugs," said Josie.

Mary agreed to do the same and all three of the boys joined them in pledging to tell everything and to stop doing drugs immediately.

Fred offered to give them any help they needed or wanted in accomplishing those goals. He also said he would do everything he could to help them avoid major punishment as long as they kept their pledges and never did either drugs or picking on other students again.

All profusely thanked Fred for what he had done and foe the fact he was willing to help them.

--- --- ---

Six years later as all of them graduated from college they had demonstrated the greatness of Fred's work in setting them on a straight path. He had made them realize where they were headed and shown them they needed to change their ways, which they had accomplished.

All had graduated in the top ten percent of their class, and all had good jobs waiting for them. After each of them accepted their diploma they turned back to where Fred was and gave him a huge hug, expressing their thanks for everything he had done.

BAD IN TOWN

D r. Fred Puller was really starting to enjoy the Spring break from teaching as he headed towards his favorite restaurant. As soon as he walked into the restaurant, he knew something was wrong. He had been eating in this restaurant for years and it had always been a quiet place to enjoy a good meal. The school where he taught, Phillip Johnson High School, was nearby. As he looked around the dining room, he saw two men at one of the tables who were apparently having an intense argument and doing their best to not be noticed. It was obvious to Fred every person in the room was aware of the argument and doing their best not to show it.

Fred was sure he had seen one of the men's picture in the paper recently. As he walked over to a table in the back of the room, he kept trying to remember what the paper had said. He mumbled to himself, "It was in the paper only three or four days ago. Why can't I remember what it was?"

As he sat down at the table, it struck him. The article had said the man he recognized was a member of a local criminal gang. Fred also remembered the article had said the man was suspected of being involved in several criminal actions, among them being gun running, extortion, and possibly bank robbery.

Fred wondered why they would sit in a public place, argue, and attract attention to themselves. Maybe, he wondered, they felt they didn't have to worry about the police. He finally decided if they didn't pull out guns, he should just keep to himself, eat, and go on home.

As Fred ate his lunch he noticed the arguing getting louder and the two men starting to get a lot more physical in their arguing. It appeared their discussion was going to get much more violent. Just as Fred was preparing to pay his bill, the two men jumped up and took positions as if they were going to fight. Their voices got loud enough for everyone in the restaurant to hear. Fred decided his best choice was to stay quiet and not attract any attention himself. The two men were arguing about money, specifically money one of them had acquired two days earlier. One man, the older of the two, made several comments about the fact the other man had not divided the money equally.

"I planned this whole thing. I know how much money was there. I did not get my half, which would be $50,000. Cough it up," the older man said.

"I took the risk on this job. I deserve the larger portion. I gave you what you deserve," The younger man replied.

"We'll see about that."

Finally both men stopped, looked around the room at all of the people staring at them. They threw some money on the table, and hurried out of the restaurant. The waitress walked over to the table, picked up the money, counted it, and turned to go back to the kitchen. "Another great tip," she said. "I wish those two would come more often."

As Fred headed out the front door, after paying his bill, he started thinking, 'I know a lot of information now on some recent crime. I know who planned it, how much was taken, the robbery itself was pulled by one man. All of this adds up to the fact I should keep my nose to myself. If I do so the perpetrators may never get caught. My God, how do I handle this and stay alive. I can't just tuck it into my memory and try to forget it'.

All the way home he kept rolling everything over in his mind. He felt he had to do something. But how to do it so he wouldn't be killed in the process. Finally he struck on a plan that might be feasible.

The next morning Fred hurried to get his morning paper to see if it had anything about a crime fitting what he knew. Sure enough, on page one, there was a story about a bank robbery. The article said a man walked into the bank, showed a gun to the tellers, and told them to get down on the floor. He then proceeded to pull open the safe door, which was unlocked in expectation of the armored van coming in less than fifteen minutes. The tellers said it contained three days of deposits and they were finishing getting it together for pickup. The robber grabbed three full bags of cash. He then went back out the front door and headed down the street. He disappeared around the corner. The employees did not try to pursue him since he had waved a pistol at them when he first entered the bank. When the police arrived they did a general search of the area and found the safe in an alley, with all of the money missing. The police speculated that the robber knew the scheduled time for the arrival of the armored van.

Fred read the story through, cut it out of the paper, and put it with the earlier article which had the pictures of the two men and their names. 'Now what to do with this. I like it here in New Orleans. I don't want to have to move to Los Angeles to save my life', he thought to himself.

Then another idea struck him. 'I can make copies of these articles and send them to the police. I don't have to write anything, just send the articles'. With that, he went back to his computer room and ran off copies of the articles. He stuffed the copies into a big envelope, and sealed it, addressed it to the local police station. He put enough stamps on it to make sure it would go through the post office. He got into his car, drove to the post office, and put it in the mail slot. On the way home, he kept asking himself, 'Have I just done something stupid? I guess I'll know when they come and shoot me'.

Finally, he tried to find something relaxing to do for the rest of the weekend. His choice, in the end, was to go to the local bookstore to browse and download a couple of books to his Nook. Two hours later, he left with four books and two e-books. He headed to another of his favorite restaurant to have lunch, all the time trying not to think of what he had done.

The next day he got up, had a small breakfast, got dressed, and went back to the bookstore to relax a bit and maybe even acquire a couple more books. After two hours of relaxing, he left and walked out to the parking lot and there he saw a true antique, a public phone booth. He headed for his car, stopped, turned around, walked over to the public phone, dropped in two quarters thinking, 'Well all they can do is kill me'.

He dialed the police department.

"The two people involved in the bank robbery yesterday are the two shown on page two of the paper from twenty August," he said.

He immediately hung up and went to his car, got in, and drove back home, with the intent of locking himself in and enjoying the next four days reading his new books. He knew he had enough food for four days, and his mail was dropped in the slot in his front door. He got a couple of his books, sat down on the sofa, and tried to stop shaking while looking for something interesting on the TV.

Four hours later, he heard the doorbell ring. His total fear returned as he peeked out the window. Two men were standing there, and Fred recognized them as the ones in the newspaper article. He went back to his sofa, sat down, and tried to decide what to do and whether he could get away through the back door. He knew he couldn't get far without his car, so he decided to sit quietly and wait. He was glad he had turned the TV off a couple of hours earlier so he could read. He sat quietly for fifteen minutes, and the two men finally left.

After it got dark, he got into his car, backed out of the driveway, and started down the street without turning his headlights on until he was three blocks away. He then turned and headed for the interstate highway intending to get at least a hundred miles away, find a motel, and stay there for a few days until he could figure out what to do.

A couple of hours later, settled into a motel, he tried to think the process through. His first thought was, 'Why did I ever stick my nose into all of this. There is a difference between doing the right thing and throwing your life away'.

Three days later as he was sitting in his motel room watching the news on TV, pictures of the two men popped up on the screen. The newscaster went into a fifteen minute detailed report on the capture of the two men, how it had happened, where, and what they were accused of doing. The newscaster then reported the police as saying they had information from two different sources connecting the two men to the bank theft. The police said they were continuing to investigate and would like anybody with additional information on this crime to call them.

Fred's instant thought was, I did that and now I'm on the run. Then he decided since the two were in jail, he probably could make a trip home, collect his mail, and see what was happening. He packed up, checked out, and started home, trying to pray for good luck the entire ninety-seven miles. As he rolled slowly down his street, approaching his house, he kept checking ahead, both sides, and in his rear view mirror, hoping he saw nothing unusual. As he pulled into his driveway, he was starting to feel reasonably safe. Everything appeared normal. He noticed several packages laying close to his front door. He knew of several things he was expecting but he decided he had better check shipping forms, carefully before he opened any of them. As he was checking the shipping forms he started wondering how the two thieves found out who had given the information to the police. He thought he had done it all anonymously. There had to be a connection somewhere to someone.

The sound of the phone ringing brought him out of his deep thought and back to his living room. He picked up the phone and heard a soft voice saying, "I work for the police department, and I wanted to fill you in on what has happened."

"Who is this? Why are you calling me? Hello? Hello?"

"My name is not important. Be quiet, just listen, and remember this. I'm going to tell you what went on and how the two thieves knew about you."

"I would really like to know."

"I told you to shut up and listen."

"OK, I will."

"Do you want to hear this or not? If you do, don't open your mouth again."

This was followed by a few moments of silence. Then the soft voice continued, "The package you mailed in had no return address so the post office stamped the zip code on it. This let the police narrow down it's source area a great deal.

"Where you phoned in the information from that street corner phone, there is a bar kitty-corner across from the where you were. They maintain a very sophisticated camera system so they can always know what is going on around them. The police managed to trace where the call came from, so they went there and talked to the bar owner to see if he had seen or heard anything that night. He told them he probably had everything recorded on his camera system. They checked the recording for the specific day and time and there you were going into and coming out of the phone booth."

"Oh my God," Fred said. "How did they find out who I was?"

"One of the policemen watching the recording said, 'I know who he is. It's Fred Puller. I live about three blocks away from him'. He promptly gave us your address. I found out later one of the cops was on the payroll of the two thieves. He had to have given them the information. That's where everything started. The cop is now in jail awaiting trial." Finally the soft voice said, "Enjoy," and quickly hung up

Fred sweated and worried for two days and finally decided to try to talk to the police chief. He phoned police headquarters and asked to talk to the chief. The woman answering the phone said, "He's very busy, too busy to talk to random callers. I can let you talk to somebody else"

Fred said, "Tell him its Fred Puller. I'm the one who supplied the information needed to solve the bank robbery. I think he'll talk to me."

A minute and a half later a man's voice came on the phone, "This is Chief Brown, what can I do for you Mr. Puller?"

"I found out what happened with my phone call. I need to discuss this whole situation with you."

"Come down to my office at four o'clock today. I'll have some time then."

"OK, see you at four."

When Fred arrived at police headquarters he was quickly ushered into the chief's office. As they talked, it became apparent to Fred that the chief was prepared to do almost anything to help him out of this situation, basically because one of his men had created all of the problems.

Four days later, Fred answered his phone and it was Chief Brown.

"You will hear all of this on the news later today, but I thought I would call you and give you the information now. We had an incident at the jail about an hour ago. Our crooked cop managed to overpower the jailer and get his gun and the keys to the cells. He released the two crooks and then they tried to shoot their way out of the jail. Four other cops took them on and all three were shot dead rather than surrender. Two of the four officers were wounded but not seriously. It looks like your troubles are over. Why don't you join me at dinner next week, so we can talk all of this over."

"You're on. Pick the day."

"Thursday at The Brownstone. Twelve noon."

"Great," was all Fred could say. "Now maybe I could can get back to my mundane normal life."

BAD IN THE STREETS

D r. Fred Puller was sitting in his classroom grading test papers. The principal, John Rausch, came in and said, "Fred, we have to talk. Something is going on."

"Something here at school?" Fred asked.

"No. Not that we know of. I've been told there's a young boy living on the streets in this area. I'm also told he is stealing food wherever he can. What he does when it rains no one seems to know. The police have been trying to catch up with him for quite some time now, but he seems to have numerous hiding places."

Fred responded, "I've never heard anything about this in the newspapers or on TV. You'd think it would be a significant news item. Is there anything I can do to help the situation?"

"No, I don't think so. It has to be up to the police right now," said the principal.

"But if it were mentioned on the TV news, it might encourage people to report seeing something. Otherwise they just think it's a boy going around town."

The principal replied, "Yes, it probably would, but the police want to keep it quiet while they search for him, so he doesn't push a panic button and try to run for it. His trying to move somewhere else could be very difficult and dangerous for him."

"Yes, that's probably true. I'll keep my eyes open. Do they know what he's wearing?"

"Not really. That makes it harder to catch up with him. All we can do is keep on the lookout for him." Rausch headed back to his office.

After another hour Fred had finished grading all of the tests and was pleased he had ninety percent of the class with a grade of B or better. He thought to himself, *I must be doing something right. Thank goodness.* He decided his next move would be to get some supper. One of his favorite restaurants was only a few blocks away, across from a city park. He packed the papers up, put them in his briefcase and headed out the door. As he passed the principal's office he gave a shout of 'Goodbye', and when he got no answer he assumed Rausch had already gone home.

The story of the young boy kept running through Fred's mind as he headed for the restaurant. His eyes kept moving back and forth as if he expected to see the youngster as he was driving along.

Fred pulled into the restaurant parking lot, went in, and got a nice table on the patio overlooking the street. He placed his order for parmesan chicken and macaroni and cheese. As he waited he looked around at the other tables and watched the cars go by. When he turned from the tables to the street he noticed a boy crossing the street. The boy came into the patio area and as he walked around Fred noticed him picking up leftover food, eating some and pocketing some.

Fred knew almost for a certainty this was the boy the police were looking for. He didn't want to scare him since he was fairly close, so he pulled out his cell phone and dialed 911. Just as he got an answer he turned and saw the boy run back across the street to the park.

"I need to report a lost boy."

"Do you know where he is now?"

"Yes. I saw him go into Central Park. He was taking food off tables here at Duncan's Steak House, then he ran back across the street and disappeared among the trees in the park. I know the police are looking for him and they need to get here as fast as they can."

The 911 operator assured Fred the police were on the way.

Very quickly a police car pulled up to the steak house parking lot and two policemen went in looking for Fred. They talked for a short time. They wanted to know what the boy looked like what clothes he was wearing, how tall he was, and the color of his hair. All this information would be included in their report. Then the policemen went across the street to search through the park.

After a while, the officers came walking out of the park, but the boy was not with them. They came back into the restaurant to talk to Fred some more.

They asked Fred, "How did you know about the boy?"

"The principal at my school told me about him. He had been briefed by someone from the police department."

"I knew some of our people were contacting various people about the boy in an effort to widen our search. Apparently it's working."

After he finished eating, Fred headed for the mall, which was only three blocks away. He didn't really enjoy shopping and particularly at a mall, but he felt he had no choice this time. He badly needed some new shirts and underwear. He encountered his first dislike when he reached the mall, finding a decent parking place. After driving around for several minutes, he finally found a place.

Fred walked briskly to the mall and through the automatic doors. He knew where the Beermans store was sand he headed there. The men's department was on the second floor, so he started for the escalator. As he passed through the women's jewelry section he glanced to his right and saw somebody he knew. He walked that way and said, "Patricia Patterson, how are you doing? I haven't seen you since they closed that bank robbery where you and I provided information on the perpetrators."

Patricia turned and smiled. "Dr. Fred. Hi. How have you been doing? It's good to see you again."

"It's good to see you too. Would you like to join me for a cup of coffee and a piece of pie. We can discuss the results of that case."

"I would love to have some pie and coffee. It will boost my energy for the rest of my shopping."

As they sat enjoying their snack and each other's company, Fred noticed the boy he had seen earlier at the cafeteria. Fred watched him closely out of the corner of his eye, not wanting to alarm him. He saw the boy walk over to a table that hadn't been cleaned up yet. The boy's eyes darted around then he quickly grabbed a half-sandwich off of a plate. He went to the front door, and headed back across the street. Fred excused himself, went over to the window, and saw the boy sitting on the bench at the bus stop. He was wolfing down the sandwich. Fred went back to their table and explained to Patricia what was happening with the boy.

"Why don't we go out front and see if we can get some information about him," Patricia said. "Maybe we can get a chance to talk to him. We could ask him something like,' Do you know where such and such is.'"

"That might work. We can go try it."

"Yes, and maybe we'll get a chance to see if he needs help."

Fred paid the tab and they went out the door and headed towards the bus stop, chatting away as if nothing important was happening. When they reached the bus stop Patricia asked the boy, "Do you know the number of the bus that goes to Fountain Avenue?"

The boy looked at them nervously for a second, decided they were harmless, and said, "I really don't know. You'll need to ask the bus driver."

"OK. Can we join you on the bench while we wait?" Fred asked.

"Sure."

Fred and Patricia sat down and gingerly entered into conversation with the boy. He asked, "How is your sandwich?"

"It's pretty small. I could sure use another one."

"I'll tell you what. These buses run slow. We were talking about getting some more coffee. Would you like to join us? We'll buy you another sandwich. OK?"

The boy got a very scared look on his face and looked like he was going to get up and run, but the idea of another sandwich on his nearly empty stomach started to take over.

"I...I...I sure would like another sandwich and something to drink."

"Great. Why don't you join us? We'll sit where we can see a bus coming."

All three went back to the restaurant, got a table near the windows. Fred and Patricia just got coffee while the boy ordered a full meal. While they waited Patricia asked, "What's your name and how old are you?"

The boy said, "My name is Roger and I'm ten years old."

Fred asked, "Do you live near here? Are your parents picking you up?"

At that question the boy started to cry.

Patricia asked, "What's wrong? Can we help you somehow?"

Roger replied, "I don't know where my parents are."

"I was at camp. The bus brought us back, dropped everyone off where their parents were supposed to pick them up. I waited there for a day. Then I really needed something to eat. I've been sleeping in the park," Roger explained, while crying harder.

"You mean you've been living on the streets? For how long?"

"Yes, sir. It's been almost a month now."

"Will you let us help you?" Patricia asked.

"Yes. I don't know what to do."

"The first thing we have to do is notify the authorities. The second thing is to make sure you have a safe, warm, comfortable place to stay. Then we can find your parents and see what happened to them."

Fred pulled out his cellphone and dialed the police department. When it was answered he said, "I am Fred Puller and I have found the boy you have been looking for. He's with me at Duncan's Steakhouse. We found him in this area. He's currently having a good meal. We will wait for you here."

Very shortly two police cars pulled up at the curb, three policemen jumped out and entered the steakhouse. Fred waved at them to attract their attention. They approached, pulled up some chairs and said, "Tell us what happened."

While two of the policemen talked to Patricia and the boy, the third one took Fred aside to talk to him.

The policeman said, "We are extremely glad you found the boy and convinced him not to run away. However you did it, we owe you a giant thanks. While the boy was in camp his parents and older sister were killed in a house fire. It's extremely tragic. We need to inform him what has happened to his family. This is always very difficult. We'll have to inform him of the tragedy? We are prepared to do whatever is necessary on his behalf."

Fred replied, "I feel he is starting to trust me. I've really just met him but, if necessary, he can stay at my place for now. The lady with me, Patricia, might be willing to help me take care of him. At least I hope so."

Patricia nodded her head in a yes motion, starting to smile at it all.

"That sounds good. It will be a big help. We'll have to clear all of this through the court, but that can be done tomorrow. I remember Patricia from both of you working with us on the bank robbery case. I see the two of you are apparently still seeing each other."

Fred fumbled and appeared to blush slightly as he said, "Oh, we're not seeing each other, though she is a very attractive and intelligent woman."

They joined the others at the table and explained what was going on. Fred spent some time talking with Roger and Patricia. Finally the policeman said, "Roger, I have to talk to you about something. It isn't pleasant, but I must tell you about it. While you were in camp, there was a fire at your home. Your parents and your sister could not get out."

"Are they OK?"

"No. I feel really bad about this but I must tell you all three of them were killed."

With that Roger started crying again. Patricia reached over and hugged him tightly. She, also, was crying. The two of them sat there hugging and crying for several minutes. Finally Roger pulled away, looked at the policeman and asked, "Where are they now? Can I see them?"

The policeman commented, "We can take you to their gravesites." He then invited Fred and Patricia to join them.

They both said yes and volunteered to follow the policemen in Fred's car.

They formed a caravan of the police cars followed by Fred's car and went to the graveyard which was about five miles away. At the graveyard they went to the graves and stood there staring.

Finally Roger turned to one of the policemen and asked, "What happens to me now?"

The policeman replied, "We'll go into court tomorrow to talk to the judge and try to get some things settled. During this time we'll take care of you. In the meantime, would you like to spend a few nights at Dr. Puller's house? You'll be safe there."

Roger looked at Fred, looked away, looked back, and nodded his head yes.

Fred said, "Let me know what time he is scheduled for court. I'll have him there. I'll probably take him shopping for some new clothes tonight. How would you like that, Roger?"

Roger apparently liked that because for the first time smiled, then he stepped over and stood between Fred and Patricia.

After viewing the graves a little longer, Fred gave the police his cell phone number. Fred, Patricia and Roger got into Fred's car and headed back to the mall. There they dropped Patricia off at her car and headed for Fred's house to get Roger cleaned up.

At Fred's place he dug out a too-long bathrobe and got Roger into the shower with instructions to clean up. While that was occurring Fred threw Roger's clothes into the washer. After the shower, and clean clothes, Roger looked almost decent again.

A little while later, Fred fixed some supper for the two of them. Halfway through supper the doorbell rang. Fred went to the door and there stood Patricia.

"Hi, how are things going?"

"We're doing as well as could be expected at this time. Come on in."

"I've seen how you dress sometimes so I figured you would need some help getting new clothes and everything for Roger."

Fred grimaced, then laughed, and said, "Come on. We have enough food for you to eat with us."

Patricia joined them at the table and when they finished they headed for the mall. At one of the big department stores, they quickly found four sets of clothes, clean underwear, plus night clothes for Roger, and headed back to Fred's place. Patricia asked Fred to let her know the court time as soon as he found out and then then got her car and left for home.

Early the next morning Fred got a phone call telling him to have Roger at the courthouse at 2:00 pm. He called Patricia and told her. She said she would see them there.

At 2:00 p.m. one of the policemen, Fred, Patricia and Roger were all seated in Judge Howard's court waiting to be called.

At 2:30 the judge asked the bailiff to bring them forward. Everyone was introduced to the judge and their presentations started.

The police officer went through the details of the case. Next Fred told how he got involved, how he had found the boy, and what he had done. He also talked about Roger staying with him. Patricia explained her involvement and added she worked part-time at 'Going Home', an agency involved in finding foster homes for homeless kids.

The judge acknowledged that information would come in handy. He asked Patricia" With your experience can you go ahead and do some lead-in studies on this matter."

She said she could.

Then the judge asked Roger, "Can you step forward and explain what has been happening with you."

Roger said, "Yes. I have been homeless for a month and didn't know what to do. I was scared of people and hungry. I didn't know where my parents were or what had happened to them. He's the one who took me in yesterday so I would have a place to eat and sleep."

"All right. I think I now have a more complete understanding of all of this. Roger, are you happy staying with Dr. Puller for now?"

"Yes, sir. He has a nice warm home, good food, and the dog next door enjoys playing with me."

Next Judge Howard asked, "Miss Patterson, can you give me some sort of idea of how long it might take to find some reasonable foster homes to choose from for Roger?"

"Give me a week and I can have something for you.", replied Patricia.

"All right. I want to see all of you back here next Monday at 2:00 pm again." At that the judge rapped his gavel and said, "Next."

The following Monday, everyone showed up in court. Along with Fred, Patricia and Roger, there was a man and a woman sitting there waiting. Patricia went over to them and said hello. She chatted with them for a couple of minutes until the judge banged his gavel and said, "Will everyone involved with the lost boy case come forward." The new couple started to get up but Patricia motioned for them to stay where they were.

Fred spoke first saying, "Roger has spent the week with me. He is an impressive young man. He is bright, a quick learner. He is always glad to pitch in and help with something. He should easily fit in with a foster family. I am qualified to foster children and I would take him in, but my time is required greatly at school and he might be left by himself a lot of times."

The judge thanked him for his comments and his honesty. He asked Patricia what she had found out.

Patricia came forward saying, "Your Honor, I have spent a lot of time on this, checking out several families. I think I have found the ideal foster family for Roger. I would like to introduce Mr. And Mrs. Alberson." She turned and indicated for the couple to come forward.

When the couple faced the judge, Mr. Alberson said, "Your Honor, my wife and I live a few blocks from Dr. Puller. We have been married for fifteen years. I work at the McBell Insurance Company. We have two boys, eleven and thirteen. We have all been over to Dr. Puller's twice this past week and our boys really took to Roger. Roger really enjoyed spending time with our boys. They have quite a few of the same interests. I think our family could provide a real home for Roger.

"From what I have heard I think I agree with you, but first I must ask Roger if he would agree with that. Roger would you step forward, and the rest of you go to the back of the room so I can talk to Roger privately."

As everybody complied, the judge stepped down from the bench and approached Roger. The judge quietly asked Him, "What do you think of everything you have heard, Roger?"

"I really enjoy being with George and Harry, their two boys. We even like the same TV shows. I enjoyed staying with Mr. Fred, but he was in and out a lot. Sometimes Miss Patricia would come over and stay with me, but not always."

"If I offered you a chance to live permanently with the Albersons, would that be OK with you?"

"Yes sir. It would be fine with me."

"Then, so be it. I will tell everybody, or would you like to do that?"

"I can do it, Sir."

The judge called everybody back to the bench and said, "Listen up. Roger has something to say."

Roger stood up straight and with a great big smile on his face said, "George, Harry and I are going to be in the same family. Mister Judge said so."

The judge stated, "The Albersons will be the foster family for Roger. This matter is settled."

It took only a couple of hours to pack up Roger's stuff and move it all to the Albersons. While Roger, George and Harry settled into getting really involved with each other, the Albersons, Fred and Patricia sat and discussed everything that had happened. Finally at 6:30 Fred and Patricia said goodbye, told Roger they would be over often to see him, and headed back to Fred's place.

As they drove the five blocks back Fred commented, "Well Patricia, I think Roger has found a great home. You know, you and I really work well together. Maybe we need to follow up on that."

Patricia didn't answer, she just looked away and smiled. She thought to herself, *Well he finally realizes that.* She looked back at Fred and thought, *He'll make a great father."*

BAD IN MEDICINE

"Well, Honey", Fred said as he handed his wife a bouquet of a dozen roses, "we've been married for almost two years now. I hope it's been as good for you as it has been for me."

"Oh Fred, they're lovely. Yes, Fred, it has been good. I've really enjoyed our being together. I'm glad you got involved in the legal action against my former employer, Brandor Manufacturing, otherwise I might never have met you."

"I know my life has been improved since I met you," Fred said.

"You have to say that since I'm pregnant. Are you going to drive me to my doctor's appointment? It shouldn't take too long since it's just a general checkup."

"Since you're pregnant with twins, it might be a fairly thorough checkup. Let's plan on leaving about nine-thirty. I've got a couple of quick errands to take care of so I'll drop you at the doctor's office and go pick up some things for my class on Friday. The students will need them."

"You really enjoy this class you're teaching now."

"Yes. It's a smaller class with only twenty students, not the usual thirty-five to forty." Fred glanced at his watch, looked up and said, "Why don't we head for the doctor's office now?"

"Okay. Let's go."

A little later, Patricia was checking in at the doctor's reception desk and Fred was making his supplies run. After checking in, Patricia waited only a few minutes before a nurse came in and called, "Patricia Puller". She was led to a curtain enclosed waiting room. While she waited, she heard someone enter the room. They stood there chatting. It turned out to be two nurses.

The first nurse said, "Have you heard the rumor about Dr. Hartman?"

The second nurse replied, "Yes. I don't know if they're true or not."

"I have actually overhead telephone conversations and people talking who are apparently involved in criminal actions."

"One of our doctors?"

"Oh, yes, and others. Believe me, this could be really bad. They mentioned fraudulent prescriptions and illegal drugs; marijuana, methamphetamine and heroin were specifically mentioned. I don't know what to do, if anything, about what I heard."

In the curtain enclosed waiting room, Patricia made sure she stayed absolutely quiet, no noise and no movement, until she heard the nurses leave the room.

Fifteen minutes later her doctor came in to examine her. "Good morning, Dr. Brown. How are you today?"

"I'm fine, Patricia, but more important, how are you?"

"I'm doing well. Some minor aches and pains are showing up."

"Well, that's to be expected when you're pregnant with twins. Are you eating well and getting enough fluids?"

"I think so."

"Let's talk while I examine you."

Dr. Brown did a complete examination of Patricia, while asking her lots of questions. At the end of the exam he said he had found nothing abnormal and told her to go home and relax. The thought that popped into her head was, 'Yeah. Like I could relax with what I just heard in this room'.

Patricia only had to wait a few minutes for Fred to return. On the way home she kept running what to do through her mind without coming up with any good ideas.

"Fred, I have to talk to you about something."

"Nothing wrong with the twins, I hope."

"No. The doctor said everything seems to be fine with all of us. This is about something I overheard while I was waiting for him. Some of the nurses were discussing illegal activities about drugs going on in the office. One had actually heard it being set up."

"My God. You heard all of that?"

"Yes. They didn't know I was there."

"Let's discuss this over coffee when we get home."

As they pulled into the garage, Fred turned to Patricia and said, "As you know I've gone through this kind of thing before, and I've found the critical thing is to find a witness willing to talk. Can you think of anyone who might do this?"

"The only one would be the nurse who overheard the phone conversation. I was, basically, in hiding and all I know is what her voice sounded like. She had an accent, I am not sure what country or area, but I would recognize it if I heard it again."

"The other problem is, it's your doctor's office. You could lose him completely. Have you considered what you would do?"

"No. I haven't, but if he's involved in all of this, I don't want him caring for me or our babies"

Three weeks later Patricia received a letter saying Dr. Brown was moving to a new office. He was teaming up with another doctor who had an established office and more business than he could handle. The letter stated he hoped Patricia would stay with him at his new office. She showed the letter to Fred and his immediate response was, "Well, one possible problem is taken care of. Now we really need to talk about what to do."

As Fred and Patricia were sitting in the den, Fred commented, "After thinking about this thing, I think there are three options. The first one is, obviously, to just forget about the whole thing. I don't think either of us really wants to do that. Second, we try to report it anonymously, as I did once before on something else. Third, we talk to the police officer I dealt with before and got to know fairly well. My feeling right now is we go the third way."

"That's probably the best way. I hope your police officer friend will start looking into it without drawing us into it."

"We have to make sure he knows our information is strictly third hand and we have no proof beyond what we tell him."

"Agreed. Can you try to contact him, Fred?"

"Will do."

The next day Fred called the police department and asked to speak to Detective Allen. He was told, "Wait a minute."

A voice came on saying, "This is Detective John Allen. What can I do for you?'

This is Dr. Fred Puller."

"Hello, Dr. Puller. How are you doing?"

Fred replied, "I'm doing fine, John. I have something to discuss with you. Could we meet over lunch sometime soon?"

"Certainly. Today would be great. I just finished some things I had to do and I will be essentially free for a couple of hours."

"Great, how about noon at that new seafood restaurant 'Chez Bon'. I think it's only a couple of blocks from your place of work."

"Sounds good. See you there at noon."

At noon as Fred walked into the restaurant, he spotted John in a booth near the back, walked over, greeted him, and sat down.

"Let's order food and then we can talk," Fred said.

After the waitress walked away from their table the detective asked, "Now, what can I do for you?"

"My wife overheard a conversation that alluded to several forms of criminal action. She was at her doctor's office when she heard two nurses discussing these activities. One of the nurses had heard someone on the phone trying to schedule a delivery of illegal drugs."

"Is this the only information you have at this point?"

"Yes, it is. I was hoping you could tap their phone or whatever you can do to get more information."

"I'll have to talk to my superior to make sure of what we can do. There are rules we have to follow."

"Yes, I know," Fred replied.

Fred then proceeded to give Detective Allen the name of the medical office, its address, and its main phone number.

"If that's the number they were calling from, it would be easy to tap it. If they were using a private phone, it becomes more difficult. I'll talk to my superior captain and we'll make some decisions."

"Please don't get my name in the mix. My wife is three months pregnant and it could create major problems for us."

"I'll do my best, but both of you may still have to talk to my superior."

"We will if it's absolutely necessary."

Finally they ate their lunch and went their separate ways.

Two days later Fred got a phone call from Detective Allen.

"I've talked to the captain and he says we need more detailed information before we can act. He wants to meet with you and your wife to try to get some answers we need."

"Not a problem but it would have to be in someplace away from the police station. How about in the city park on Broad Street?"

"Sounds good. How about Tuesday at noon?"

"Great. I don't have any classes Tuesday, and Patricia is available then. See you there."

On Tuesday Fred and Patricia pulled into the parking lot and saw Detective Allen sitting on a bench with another man. As they walked over to them, Fred noticed they had a piece of paper, and assumed it was a listing of the things they wanted answered."

As Fred and Patricia walked up to the bench, Detective Allen introduced them to the other man. "This is Chief Johnson, Bill Johnson. Please sit down and we can talk."

"We have discussed this at length and we have a few questions for you", he said, as he referred to the notes on the paper."

Detective Allen and Chief Johnson went through their list, making sure they got detailed answers as to what went on. After nearly an hour they seemed quite pleased with the information they had gotten. They told Fred and Patricia they could go on home, Detective Allen would contact them as soon as a decision was made.

Later, Detective Allen called to tell Fred the data they had provided was enough to justify tapping the phones at the medical center. It was found there were three different phone numbers, one used only at the receptionist's desk, a second was only for the doctor's use, and a third for general use. Phones one and two showed no unusual activity, but from the third one they had obtained a great deal of information. They were now proceeding with legal action against two doctors, three nurses, and one handyman.

Fred immediately asked if Dr. Brown was one of the two doctors they had information on. The reply was, "No. Dr. Brown was not involved at all."

Fred's response was, "Great. Patricia will be greatly relieved."

Fred went quickly to tell Patricia what Detective Allen had told him about Dr. Brown.

"Oh, thank goodness. I don't have to change doctors," was Patricia's comment.

Three days later the headlines in the paper and on TV was about the raid on the medical center, and the arrest of six people. Detective Allen was extensively quoted, "We found records of selling of cocaine, heroin, and marijuana, along with methamphetamine. In addition there were illegal sales of prescription drugs. We're certain we have enough data to charge all of them and I don't foresee any problem with finding all six of them guilty. Three of the people had confessed.

Fred and Patricia never mentioned anything about all of this again, just to be safe.

SAVING THEM

As Bob sat at his kitchen table having breakfast a thought popped into his head, *This was going to be a tremendous day for a walk in the woods*. The paper had said it was to be mid 70's, full sunshine, and just a very light breeze. He had been thinking of walking the trail through a wooded area about ten miles from his home. The trail made a long loop through the woods, was about four miles long, and there usually was very few other people around. That was the length of walk he needed and this was going to be the perfect day for it. He had been working late every night for five weeks and had not been able to go for a walk. He decided he was going to use the day to catch up and the best part was he could finally take a day off work for it.

In his mind the decision had already been made and all he had to do was get things together and go. He planned on hitting the woods by 9:30 am. With that settled, breakfast went down quickly. Bob got dressed and rushed around to collect everything he would need for the day: a water bottle, snack bars and, finally, his hiking stick.

Even though he was seventy-five he had no qualms about doing a four mile hike. He had been active all his life. This included hiking, along with regular rounds of tennis, golf, plus senior's softball games.

A little after nine a.m. he climbed into his car and fifteen minutes later he pulled into the parking area that allowed access to the trail. He put on the small backpack containing his water and snacks, and prepared to enjoy the view as he walked. He started down the trail. He knew he was going to thoroughly enjoy this walk. His mind focused on enjoying all the scenery, the little animals, the birds, and the occasional deer he came across.

Bob was a mile and a half into the walk when he heard voices coming up behind him. He didn't want to be bothered with other people so he ducked off the trail into the woods and waited behind a large tree. As the voices got closer he noticed it sounded like a lot of people. He was glad he was letting them go on their way.

Being curious about the group, Bob peeked around the tree as they went past. He saw three men with a group of eight young girls. They appeared to be around five to seven years old. The men started pushing the three youngest looking girls, telling them to go faster or they would be severely punished. They were told to keep up with the other girls.

The men spoke with an accent Bob didn't recognize. The three girls started to cry and to ask the men to take them home. They said they wanted their mothers and fathers and they were getting tired. One of the men, very harshly, said for them to move it and started getting rougher with them. Another of the men brandished a gun, pointing it at the girls. The girls started walking a little faster, still crying.

Bob realized the girls must have been kidnapped and were probably headed to a life of pure hell if something wasn't done. He knew, at this point, the something was up to him. But what? He regretted he had not brought his cell phone with him, but on long hikes he never wanted his office trying to call him. He was now realizing he should carry it but just keep it turned off.

Bob decided to stay hidden and follow them at a reasonable distance in order to see what was really going on and what he could do about it.

With that decision he headed out, staying in the woods as deep as was necessary while trying to keep an eye, or at least an ear, on the group. It went this way for about three-fourths of a mile and then one of the men dropped off, said something in their language, waved them to go on, and headed into the woods. Bob was afraid he had been spotted, but the guy only went about fifteen feet into the woods and stopped at one of the trees. It became obvious that he needed to relieve himself. Bob felt he had to do something soon but he knew that caution was the primary need. He snuck up in back of the man, trying to keep very quiet. He knew his heavy walking stick could be an excellent weapon.

When he got about four feet behind the guy, the guy started to turn around while zipping up his pants. Then he saw Bob. His eyes popped wide open, and he reached in his pocket. Bob swung the walking stick and struck him on the side of the head with the heavy metal end. The guy dropped straight to the ground and didn't move. Bob waited about thirty seconds, ready to swing again if necessary, but the guy still didn't move and it was apparent he would probably never move again.

Bob kissed the end of his walking stick and quietly said "Thank you. You're worth every penny I paid for you." Then he reached into the guy's pocket and pulled out a pistol. He checked to see if it was fully loaded, made sure the safety was on, and put it in his pocket.

Then he started out in the direction the other two men had gone with the little girls. He could still hear them talking in the distance up ahead of him.

Now he had to figure out what to do next. At least now he had a gun if it became needed. The only question was would he really use it. After killing the first guy, he was certain he would have no choice. He knew he would do everything necessary to rescue those girls. He also understood he didn't have a lot of time to accomplish that goal or they would all disappear to only they knew where.

He moved a little quicker and closer on the trail to catch up to where he could see the other men while still staying quiet so they wouldn't hear him. The two of them were talking and laughing and probably couldn't hear him even if he got closer.

Suddenly the two guys stopped and took off a backpack one of them had on. They sat down at one of the larger trees and ordered the eight girls to sit down in the grass around the tree. They then pulled out some cans of beer and some sandwiches and proceeded to relax for a bit. They did not offer the girls anything despite their pleading and crying.

Bob knew they were only about a half-mile from where a road passed close by the trail. He felt it probably would be the last chance for him to do a rescue. But what to do? He was certain the gun would have to come into play. Finally he slowly crept up on the group.

He caught a glimpse of somebody coming and ducked behind a large tree. A few seconds later he carefully peeked around the tree and saw it was one of the two men. As the man walked past the tree, Bob could see he was only three feet away. He gently picked up his 'infamous' walking stick, quietly stepped out into the path and swung the knob end as hard as he could. The noise of the skull being fractured was so loud Bob feared the third man would hear it even though he was probably, at least, a hundred yards away.

The man he clobbered dropped to the path like a dead man. When Bob checked him, he found it was an accurate description. The skull had a two inch indentation in it.

The only thought Bob could bring up was, *Two down, one to go.* Now he had to go after the last one. He took off around the path in a fast walk. Five minutes later Bob saw the man with the girls. He was standing near where the path and road were close together and he kept looking up and down the road like he was expecting someone.

Bob stepped over into the woods and started to slowly approach the man and the young girls. The man was so intent on the road that Bob easily got within twenty feet of him without being seen or heard. Then Bob pulled out the gun he had taken off the first guy.

The girls saw Bob coming, but when he put a finger to his mouth telling them they should be quiet, they all turned away from him so they wouldn't indicate what was going on.

Bob was not sure if he could pull the trigger, particularly in front of the young girls, but he knew this could well be his only option. He took the pistol's safety off and slowly walked up behind the third man, who was still watching the road next to the path.

Bob came to about five feet behind the guy and then said, "What are you doing with those girls?"

The man jumped from shock, turned and reached for his pistol.

Bob said, "Stop. I'll shoot."

As the man continued pulling out his pistol, Bob aimed pulled the trigger. The blast of the shot rocked everyone back, but the scream of pain, as the man dropped the gun and grabbed his arm, was even more overpowering. The man turned and ran down the path as fast as he could go.

All eight of the girls scattered into the woods and hid behind trees. As the man disappeared down the path they all slowly came out and approached Bob. To reassure them, Bob grinned real big and said, "Now we need to get all of you home to your parents. Do all of you have names?" Immediately there came back, "Becky, Renee, Vicki, Wanda, Terri, Melinda, Kim, Shana" as all eight approached Bob.

"How soon can we go home?" Becky asked.

"Just as soon as I can get the police here to take over. I need to find a phone. I left my cell phone at home."

"Well, that wasn't very smart", Renee responded.

"I know. I don't need reminded. Let me try to catch someone on the road over here."

Just then a man came walking cautiously down the path. Obviously he had heard the shot. Bob, with all of the girls around him, hailed the man and asked if he had a cell phone.

At the answer of 'yes' Bob asked him if he could call 911 and ask the police to come. The man proceeded to call 911 and tell the operator what Bob was telling him. The operator immediately notified the police, urging them to hurry.

Fifteen minutes later two police cars pulled up where everybody was standing. Four policemen got out of the cars and quickly started talking to Bob to get the details of what had happened. Two of them started down the path in the direction the third man had gone. He was back in fifteen minutes without having found anything but a trail of blood. He went over to his car and told his headquarters to notify hospitals to be on the lookout for the wounded man. He gave them the description Bob had given him. The police continued talking to the girls to get as much information as possible. They also were continually relaying the information back to headquarters where they were trying to contact the parents.

Eventually eight sets of parents came to the scene. Plus, the police received a message that the guy with the gunshot wound had been found in the emergency ward of a nearby hospital. He was now under arrest and heading to jail.

Bob had just one thought, *I think I'll find someplace more public to walk in the future.*

SAVING THE BABY

John and Cindy Thompson were enjoying a leisurely walk around Lake Boko. They enjoyed walking there because the scenery was so nice and the ocean beachfront was only two hundred yards away so they could see the waves breaking on the beach while they strolled around the lake. Another thing they enjoyed at this lake was they also got to see a variety of animals, both ocean shore and lake front types.

As they walked, they heard noises up ahead of them. Curious, they picked up the pace to see what was happening. As they stepped around a stand of bushes they saw a baby robin on the edge of the lake. It was raising quite a fuss. Apparently it was just beginning to fly and had left the nest and struggled through the air for the short distance to the lake's edge.

Then the couple spotted a large grey house cat that was creeping up on the baby robin. The parent robins were in the closest tree adding a great deal of noise to the melee.

At that point John and Cindy saw a tern flying over from the beachfront to see what all the noise was about. It then proceeded to add a lot more noise while circling over the cat. Then suddenly, the tern dive bombed the cat causing it to duck down, turn, and start to run toward the covering

111

bushes. As the tern climbed back up into the air, making as much noise as he could, the cat turned and started back towards the baby robin.

The whole process started again. The yelling, the diving, the ducking, the running, and the climbing back up.

After watching the whole process being repeated, John commented, "That tern must have had good intentions because it was saving the life of the baby robin."

Cindy replied, "Yes. I agree with you."

The whole process was repeated for a third time. As the fourth round commenced, a second tern came flying in from the beach front and dove down, startling the cat, and causing him to decide his prey had too much protection so he promptly vacated the area. As the cat disappeared into the woods the robin parents flew in and, with their encouragement, got the baby to struggle back up into the tree where he would be safe.

Finally the two terns flew down and landed on the edge of the lake. They started circling, apparently looking for food or fighting. As they slowly circled each other John commented, "Those two terns have done a good job of driving that cat away and protecting the baby robin.

"Yes," said Cindy, "they did a very good job. It was nice of them."

Then they noticed that the terns were dancing around each other, not looking for food.

"I think that's a mating dance," said Cindy.

"I think you are right," John replied. "Which works out well, because one good tern deserves another."

I Can't Do That

John Hubbard was glad to have been invited to lunch with his long-time friend, Betty. They had known each other for twelve years, ever since they had met at a local conference on dealing with the government. Betty was the older of the two by seven years, but they had found they enjoyed each other's company and they had become great friends.

During lunch Betty said she needed help from John at a party she was planning for a group of politically very liberal people. A few of those coming were conservative about their politics, but there were no moderates to support the middle ground.

"John, I need you to help balance things. I know you aren't strongly liberal, but I still need you to be closer to moderate in the discussions. I know you can handle that."

"You know I can't do that. You expect me to pretend I'm a moderate for the party. I was born and raised a liberal, far left leaning, all my life."

"Please. Just this once for me. I've been planning this party for five months and I need your help to pull it off. It will be the social event of the year in this town."

"So long as I can be myself I'll do everything I can to help make it a success."

"All right, you can stay as you are, a far left liberal. I need your help that bad."

At that point John Hubbard agreed to do what he could for the party. After all he had known Betty Fortham all her life and he felt an obligation to help her out.

"Is the party going to be at your house?"

"No, John. I've rented a dance hall just outside of town on Old Marble Road. Several of the biggest Republican politicians in the state are going to be there. This really could turn out to be the biggest and most important event of the year."

"I hope you are going to have beer there. It sure improves my ability to work at anything."

"You'll be well covered, John. There'll be beer, hard liquor, plus soft drinks for those that want to stay sober, for whatever reason."

With that assurance John headed home to take care of some housecleaning he had been putting off. Dishes, sweeping, the usual stuff he had found easy to put off since his wife had left him three years ago. He still missed her, but was slowly getting over her.

As he drove along, he noticed signs advertising the local zoo. Every few corners he saw one with a different animal pictured on it. He had seen a zebra, a hippo, a kangaroo, plus several different birds, such as a hawk, an eagle, and a penguin. He thought the signs were very good advertising for the zoo. He made a mental note to go to the zoo this weekend. He had to plan on going early because of the party Saturday evening.

As he turned into his driveway he was running through the things he had to get done and hoping he would remember them all. The one sure thing he had to remember was the

Democratic get together on Friday evening. There was going to be some serious planning about the upcoming election.

Three hours later John decided enough was enough. It was time to quit cleaning and go get supper. Where? At the new Bob Evans obviously and afterwards a couple of beers at the bar next door. He usually ran into someone he knew at one or the other of the two places, or even at both of them. Of course, it was normally a Democrat because he had very few Republican friends and those were not out and out about their politics.

So, as could be expected, when he entered the bar there sat two of his Republican friends. They knew John well enough to know how to pull his chain and punch his buttons. One immediately asked him if he was going to vote for the Republican candidate. John cooperated by saying a couple of curse words, turning around and leaving the building, followed by the sounds of laughter.

At that point he headed back home, not to finish his cleaning, but because he had a six pack of beer in the fridge. He planned to have a couple and watch one of the movies he had taped off of TV, probably the 1932 Boris Karloff one, 'The Mummy'.

During the next day, Friday, John went through the day getting ready for his evening meeting. He called Betty a couple of times to clear up some details for Saturday night, but primarily he worked on his presentation for the Democratic Party meeting. Through the entire day he was still totally upset and angry about the meeting in the bar and his reaction to it. He knew he should have responded to those two instead of turning and leaving. Throughout Friday he thought of several different responses he should have made that would have put them down and embarrassed them. It was too late now, but he stayed upset all day.

At the Democratic get together John won the day with his presentation and thus convinced the group to follow his suggestions for the upcoming election. As the meeting broke up he looked forward to Betty's party, knowing he would still be upset with what had happened in the bar.

He spent Saturday morning, finishing the cleaning and laying out his best suit for the party. A shower, a shave, brush his teeth and he was ready to get dressed. He usually enjoyed this kind of thing when he didn't have any Democratic obligations waiting. Those would occur later in the week and he was really looking forward to them.

Finally he backed out of his driveway and followed the GPS directions coming in a nice, polite feminine voice, which made him wish he could really meet her instead of her just ordering him around. He knew it was probably a twenty-five minute drive to where the party was being held, so he left about forty minutes before he was due there.

As he drove along his thoughts were deep into the Democratic stuff he needed to get done. He almost missed two turns the voice told him to take. Finally he was close to Old Marble Road and the dance hall where the party was being held. As he approached the intersection he saw one of the zoo signs hanging just above a traffic sign. As he came up to the intersection he saw Old Marble Road was a one way street to the right. He also noticed the zoo sign had an elephant pictured on it and the traffic sign had an arrow pointing to the right and said 'Right Turn Only'. At the turn John's hands started to shake and he sailed right through the intersection. Once through it he settled down and decided he would go on down the road, turn around, come back, and make a left turn on the road he wanted to take. That way the signs would show a picture of an elephant and a 'Left Turn Only' sign.

Three miles down the road he came upon a line of cars backed up at an accident. It took twenty-five minutes to clear the accident and open up the road. John finally found a place to turn around two miles farther down the road. Once turned around, he sped back the five miles to Old Marble Road, made his left turn and hurried on down to the parking lot for the dance hall. He hopped out and ran in, noting he was over a half hour late. Just inside the door he found a bunch of people and Betty standing there with her hands on her hips and a wild look in her eye.

"Where in the Devil have you been? You know I really needed you here before people arrived. You're late and you've created a major problem for me since I had to do a lot of your stuff as well as all of mine, and still greet the arrivals as they came. I'm extremely upset in case you hadn't noticed," said Betty in a low and angry voice. "Where have you been?"

John proceeded to tell her the story of the two signs and the fact he couldn't force his hands to turn the steering wheel at the combination of the elephant and right turn only signs. Betty told him he was no longer needed and he should go back home. She also said he was lucky it was a left hand turn or he would never get home because those zoo elephant signs were all over town.

THE RING

"**O**h God, I'm late. I'm so late," John kept telling himself. "Rebecca will be really ticked off. Probably worse than ticked off. I'm in so much trouble. She'll never forgive me. She's been planning this special dinner for four months now, and my boss picked today to tell me I had to work late to reach a point where they could finish the contract. He made sure I understood it meant a great deal to the company and had to be finished on time. Then he stayed in the room with me and I couldn't even call my wife and tell her what was going on. Plus, her birthday is in two weeks. I really need to do something great to make up for this."

"I got her those three scarves she said she had to have, but with this I will have to go way beyond three scarves. Maybe I'll get her a really nice piece of jewelry to go with the scarves. I know of a jewelry store downtown with some nice things, although they were quite expensive. Sometime next week I'll have to go down there to see what they have. I can only hope all I will have done is enough for her to forgive me. If it isn't, I can give up any idea of 'cuddling' for the next six months. Maybe longer."

As it turned out, he got home just before any of the ten guests arrived. This absolved him of a large part of the trouble he was in with Rebecca. Of course, Rebecca insisted there were several things still to be discussed, but since he blamed the whole problem on his boss, the discussion was quite short, and later he found out it didn't affect the cuddling one bit.

The next day his boss told him he had to work through his lunch hour the next three days to assure meeting the deadline on the contract.

By noon of the third day, the contract was done and ready to go out. His boss said there could be a bonus in his next paycheck.

John immediately asked, "Can I also have a longer lunch hour today to take care of some vital business?"

"Yes. I think we can handle that now. I plan on taking a longer lunch break and take my wife to a nice restaurant to celebrate. So go, now. Get out of here."

John rushed out the door. His goal was to have a quick bite to eat and then head downtown to the jewelry store which had all of the nice, expensive stuff. As he pulled out of the parking lot, his first stop would be at the restaurant, five blocks away.

After a burger, fries, and some coffee, he headed downtown. About halfway there he spotted a sign saying, 'Moving sale. Everything must go. Furniture, Clothes, Tools, Jewelry'.

John said, "Tools and jewelry. I have to stop and see what they have."

A block down the side street there was a house with the front yard full of tables covered with stuff. John pulled up to the curb, hopped out of his car, and strolled over. He noticed they were just bringing out a bunch of tools and jewelry. He was heading for the tools, when he glanced at the table containing the jewelry.

"Hmm, there is some nice looking stuff there. I guess I'll browse through it first."

A woman was standing there keeping an eye on things.

"Why are you getting rid of all this nice stuff?" John asked.

"All of this was originally belonged to my husband's grandmother. She passed away ten years ago and these things have just been collecting dust since then. She bought most of them before my husband was born, which goes back a lot longer than I care to mention. We decided this moving sale was a great time to see if we could get a little money for it."

"Well let me browse through it for a bit."

"Be my guest."

John shuffled through the rings with the lady standing ready. He finally picked out what appeared to be a large fake diamond. He examined it closely. Then he thought, "Why am I examining this thing. I don't know squat about rings."

He looked at a couple of other rings and some necklaces before he decided the one ring was be enough.

"How much is this ring?"

"Twenty-five dollars. There are some more there available for the same price too," she encouraged him.

"No. I think this one will do," he replied as he pulled a twenty and a five out of his wallet and paid for the ring.

As he headed back to work he thought, 'This really looks like a nice ring. I think, sometime over the next few days I'll take it someplace and get it appraised. I'll bet its worth a couple hundred dollars. Friday looks like a good day to do that.' He whistled all the way home, thinking about what a great deal he had gotten.

On Friday John could hardly wait till lunch to get the ring checked. At lunch time he dashed out the door to his car, and drove to the jewelry store, went in, and said he would like to get a ring appraised. About five minutes later the jeweler came over and said, "You wanted an appraisal?" John showed him the ring, the jeweler took it, rolled it around in his hands examining it carefully, and said, "Well, it seems to be sixteen karat gold."

At this comment John's eyes opened very wide.

Then the jeweler sat down at his worktable for a lengthy appraisal. After ten minutes of carefully examining the stone, which seemed like an eternity to John, he looked up and asked, "Where did you get this ring?"

"I just bought it for my wife at a yard sale. I thought it was just costume jewelry, but I wanted to see if it was worth anything. I wanted to see if I did the right thing."

"Well, as I first thought, it is a real half carat flawless diamond."

John suddenly felt faint. He had to sit down, while he asked, "What is it worth?"

"I would place the value around fifteen hundred dollars. Easily," the jeweler replied.

John grabbed hold of the table to keep from falling off his chair.

"I'll give you twelve hundred for it right now."

"I can't. It's a present for my wife. I think I'll go now. I'm late getting back to work," he replied.

The jeweler polished the ring with his cloth and then put it in a nice little box. He handed it to John saying, "My compliments. Enjoy."

John took the box and put it in his coat pocket. "Thank you," He gave the jeweler the twenty-dollar fee. When he got outside, he sat in his car for a few minutes, still feeling faint. While he recovered, he reached a decision. He would return the ring to the people he bought it from since they obviously did not know the value of it when they sold it to him. As he drove back to their place, he derided himself for being so honest, but he knew he would never forgive himself if he didn't do the right thing.

At their house, he went up to the door and rang the doorbell. A man opened the door. "What can I do for you?," he said gruffly.

John replied, "I bought this ring from your yard sale---"

"You bought it, you own it. We don't accept returns. We do not return money. Now get out of here," the man said as he slammed the door in John's face. John was shocked as he heard the deadbolt lock click into place.

John stood there in total amazement. Finally with a shake of his head, he turned and started back down the steps to his car. He looked back and said, "I don't believe it. You try to do something nice and this is what happens. If he wants to treat me so mean, I'll just never bother him again."

Suddenly he fully realized what had happened, and he felt the urge to jump for joy. Instead he climbed into his car, and headed home.

"I guess I have a really nice diamond ring worth $1,500 to give my wife for her birthday next week."

He started driving down the street, saying "Oh, yes. Oh, yes."

The moral is: Be nice to people, it works out much better in the end.

My Love, Jennifer

It was a bright, sunny day and the sand was nicely warm, but that was not the reason I was walking slowly along the beach. This area is where my fiancé, Jennifer, was run down and killed by two teenagers racing their cars on the beach. I don't know exactly what happened, but I assume they didn't see her in time and, being on sand, could not stop readily. Actually they ran two people down and killed them. The second person was a close friend of Jennifer's. The two of them thoroughly enjoyed walking on the beach. They had done it many times and never before had any kind of problem.

Walking the beach now left me with a feeling of closeness to Jennifer. I wasn't prepared to give up the feeling. As I walked, I gave a lot of thought to her and to all of the things she usually did. She was very personable and friendly, she was on the Board of Deacons at church and was talking about joining the Trustees Board. She was very religious but also loved to tell jokes. Plays on words and puns were her favorites. She always became the center of attention at parties by telling one-liners or short jokes. She had a great sense of humor. Some of her best that I will never forget were:

1. Why is the third hand on a watch called the second hand?
2. Why is bra singular and panties plural?
3. Why do we drive on a parkway and park on a driveway?
4. A dog gave birth to puppies near a road and was cited for littering.
5. A hole has been found in the nudist colony's wall. The police are looking into it.

Just remembering these makes me miss Jennifer so much. I will miss her forever.

I continued on down the beach and as I approach the area where she was actually hit and killed the tears started to flow gently. Then I looked down and saw something partially buried in the sand. I bent over to check it out, finally picking it up. It was a Rolex watch, a very expensive looking Rolex. As I examined the watch closer, I saw words engraved on the back of it. These words said, "Your Delicious Love, Jennifer."

At that point I realized that Jennifer had bought this watch as a gift to me. I was totally overcome. I could only sit down on the sand and really start to cry. It took fifteen minutes for me to pull myself together and be able to stand up.

As I started walking I remembered some of the blonde jokes Jennifer loved to tell even though she was herself was a beautiful, highly intelligent, blonde. Some of these jokes that come to mind are:

1. Why are brunette's jokes so short? That way a blonde can understand them.
2. What are the worst three years of a blonde's life? Third grade.

3. There was a blonde who had two horses and couldn't tell them apart. She decided to cut part of one's tail off, but it grew back. She then shaved part of the horse's ear, but it grew back. She gave up and just decided to keep the white one in one barn and the black one in another.

The thing Jennifer really enjoyed doing was reading bloopers at the Church Board meetings. These bloopers actually appeared in church bulletins. She had a large collection of them and they always got the Board laughing uproariously. Some I remember are:

1. The Fasting and Prayer Conference includes meals
2. Ladies, don't forget the rummage sale. It's a chance to get rid of those things not worth keeping around the house. Bring your husbands.
3. A bean supper will be held on Tuesday evening. Music will follow.
4. The ladies of the church have cast-off clothing of every kind. They may be seen in the basement on Friday afternoon.
5. At the evening services tonight the sermon topic will be 'What is Hell?" Come early and listen to our choir.

At this point I was laughing harder than I was crying so I decided to take my gift watch home and continue to reminiscence about Jennifer and what a wonderful woman she had been. I will love her forever and I will never forget her.

I Didn't Do That

As Republican Senator Harry Belton sat at his desk going through the papers he was working on, the phone started to ring. He picked it up. "Hello. Who is this?"

"Sir, I'm Robert Harrison from the FBI office. I have George Callent from the Congressional Ethics Office here with me. We need to talk to you about some information given to us. We received a private tip raising some concern about one of your activities. We need to check and see if there is any truth in this."

"I can assure you, as a Republican Senator from the best state in the Union, I have always acted in a totally honest manner. I am extremely busy right now so I would appreciate both of you leaving me alone. Thank you."

"We can't do that, sir. This is an official investigation. If you will cooperate we could be done in less than a couple of hours. If everything turns out as you say, it should take a lot less time."

"And if I refuse to let you do this?"

"I'm afraid you don't have an option. This is officially sanctioned. Your only option is to resign from Congress."

"I have no intention of doing that. I think my work here is far too valuable to terminate. Maybe we need to talk about this. See what we can work out."

"Everything has been worked out. We need to collect this lie detector data. From what you say, it should show no problem. After that, we will leave and not bother you again."

, "I know I'm innocent," responded Congressman Belton, "so let's do this and get it over with."

"All right. If you can meet us at our office, it will be a lot easier to accomplish this."

"I just said I was extremely busy. Why can't we just do it here?"

"Our office is only three miles from yours. You can be here in less than ten minutes, take the test, and be back in your office in less than two hours. It's very important we get this done as soon as possible. We urge you to do as we ask."

"I guess I don't have much choice at this point, do I? I'll be at your office at 2 o'clock this afternoon."

"Fine. We will be all set up and ready to go when you get here. Goodbye for now."

Later in the afternoon Senator Belton headed over to the FBI office. In the three miles there were four turns in the road. At the final intersection he noticed a sign set up at the turn that had a donkey on it and advertised a donkey farm located there. The sign was right above a directional sign saying "Left Turn Only". The Senator sat there for over a minute and finally decided he could not make the turn because of the combination of signs located there. He thought to himself, I cannot force myself to obey a left turn with a donkey sign. He then proceeded straight ahead to a point where he could turn around, and headed back to his office.

When he reached his office he called and told Robert Harrison he would have to come to his office if he wanted to complete the test. He would not explain why over the phone.

An hour later Robert and George arrived at the Senator's office and rolled in the portable lie detector unit and proceeded to set it up. Harry stared at it intently and long with no expression on his face.

"How accurate is this thing? Can it be tuned to accept a false answer or miscue on a right answer?"

"Neither", said Robert. "It is set up by a team of professionals. They have been doing this for years and are very good at it. None of their machines has ever been proven wrong."

While they were discussing all of this Robert and George were connecting Harry up to the machine.

Harry finally asked, "How does this thing work?"

"It records several physiological indices such as blood pressure, pulse, respiration, and skin conductivity while you are asked and answer a series of questions," Robert answered. "A typical polygraph test starts with a pre-test interview to gain some preliminary information. The subject is asked to deliberately lie and then the tester can report he was able to properly detect a lie. Then the actual test begins. Some of the questions asked are irrelevant and the remainder are the relevant questions."*

"We will start with questions to which the answer is known, such as name, address, position," George interjected "We're ready to start now. What is your name?"

"Harry Belton," was the answer given with no response from the machine.

"Where do you live?"

"I currently reside at 1084 Borders Avenue, here in the District of Columbia. My real address is in the state of..."

Robert cut him off saying, "We don't need lengthy answers. The machine works better with short answers."

Robert continued, "What is your position?"

"I am a Republican Senator from the state of..."

Again Robert cut him off, "Please remember, short answers only."

"The machine has indicated both answers are true. Everything is as it should be. Now on the next set of questions we ask you to deliberately lie so we can see how it affects the machine. Please, just answer with a 'yes' or 'no'. First, are you nineteen years old?"

The Senator replied, "Yes, I am nineteen years old." The needle slid over indicating a lie.

"Remember, just a 'yes' or 'no' answer.

The next question was, "Have you ever cheated on your wife?"

The answer he got was, "Yes.

The needle popped way over indicating a complete lie. Robert then said, "OK. We have our range set from truth to a lie. We can now proceed with the important questions."

The Senator leaned back and tried to relax, not knowing what this set of specific questions would be.

"As a Senator," Robert opened with, "have you ever accepted money to do a favor for one of your constituents?"

Harry responded with a raised voice, "I have never done that. I would never do anything dishonest." The needle promptly went to 'LIE" Upon seeing that the Senator commented, "I think your machine is not tuned properly."

"The machine is tuned properly. The test questions proved it was. Your answer to the last question was not completely true. Let's try another question and remember only 'yes' or 'no'. Have you ever lied to a Democrat about anything?"

"Never! I always try to play fair." At that point the needle of the lie detector pegged on 'LIE'.

"Well maybe a small one, but I didn't really mean it".

"Was this just politics?"

"Yes. I really, really didn't mean it."

Again the needle inched over towards "LIE".

The Senator threw in the comment, "See. It was really just in fun."

"Okay. We will accept that," said George. "It seems to be normal in today's politics."

"Lets move on. You have lots of donors from big companies do you not?"

"Certainly. That is not something considered wrong in our business. All politicians do. They have to if they want to survive."

With this comment the needle did not move at all.

"If you are ready, the next question is, have you ever done a special favor for one of your big donors?"

"No. Never. Never."

Just as quickly the needle nearly broke in two as it hit the peg. Harry stared at the needle as he blanched and turned white in the face.

"Wait. let me rephrase the answer. I have considered it in the past but I have never actually done it."

Again the needle went to the peg but not as hard.

"Now we are at the crux of this meeting. The tip we received and which initiated all of this was that you were working on a project for your biggest donor. The result was to be his company receiving a big defense contract without open bidding."

"I deny everything," interjected Harry as the needle pegged itself again.

"Well, I think that we have all of the data we need. We'll go back to our office and proceed from there. Thank you Senator."

• per Wikipedia

GENEALOGY OF AN ORPHAN

"I don't know. I honest to God truly do not know exactly when I was born. It had to be at least twenty years ago. You only have to be eighteen years old to vote, so I don't understand why they wouldn't let me register to vote."

"You have to remember Martin, without proof of your birth date they have no choice but to turn you down. They represent the Government and could lose their job if they did it wrong."

"I understand that, Pastor Phil, but what can I do now?"

"You need to do some research on yourself. What do you know about yourself? Where were you born?"

"It was somewhere in southern Indiana is all I know. Exactly where, your guess is as good as mine. From there I was raised in about seven foster homes. The longest stay in any of them was two years. Finally, the last one declared me an adult and said I was on my own. I've just been surviving on odd jobs here and there, catch as catch can, and living anywhere I could find a spot to sleep. It's been a rough two years."

"OK, Martin. I will do all I can to help you. I think you are a good, deserving, person, and I would not feel like a true man of God if I didn't try. I am going to let you bed down at night in my church. We have a couple of rooms with sofas. You can sleep on one of those for now. I will see that you get regular meals. In the meantime stay with your jobs and I will do a little digging. I know a couple of pastors in southern Indiana who might be able to help. Have you eaten supper yet?"

"No, sir. I have money enough for a sandwich. That will hold me for tonight."

"I think I'll take you to the restaurant down on the corner and get you a full meal for once. While we eat, we can discuss the best way to approach this whole problem. Tomorrow I'll start digging into this, beginning with contacting my two preacher friends."

The next day, with Martin safely ensconced in the church, Pastor Phil placed two phone calls. One to each of his preacher friends, and set up a three way telephone meeting with them. He wanted their input on how best to find out something about Martin. He knew he had to find when and where Martin was born if at all possible. He planned on all three of them getting together on the phone on Friday to discuss the situation. This gave him three days to talk with Martin and collect everything he could remember of his early life. Hopefully it would include something on his first foster family.

Later that day he took Martin to a local restaurant for lunch. As they ate and talked, he asked all kinds of questions of Martin in order to find out how much he remembered of his early life, as well as a means of jogging his memory about his early families. Martin could recall almost all of the foster homes he had been in except for the first two or three. He had been too young to remember much about them but those were the ones where they really needed to find something. Martin wasn't even sure whether there were two or three families involved back then. His first real memories were from when he was five years old and were of a family of six, father, mother, three boys, and one girl. He was with this family for two years before being handed over to another family consisting of just husband and wife. He was with this family less than a year before they decided they weren't really cut out to be parents.

Martin assumed he had been given his name either by his birth mother at the hospital or by his first foster family. His basic assumption was his birth mother had put his name on paperwork at the hospital, so if they could trace back that far they could find out who he was and the time and place of his birth. If they found the hospital they could search on his first and middle names, 'Martin Robert'. As far back as he remembered he had those two names, even though his last name had changed many times.

The first foster homes he remembered had been in the vicinity of Indianapolis, Indiana. That should help, hopefully, to narrow the search.

"Strange you should mention Indianapolis," Pastor Phil said. I served as an assistant pastor of a church in that city for seven years and still have many contacts there. I could get in touch with a few of them and maybe we will get lucky. One of them might remember which hospitals were in that city eighteen to twenty years ago."

After eating, the two of them headed back to the church to get Martin settled in. Once there the Pastor made sure Martin had everything he needed, plus a list of tasks to accomplish before he went to bed. He went to his office, dug out his old list of phone numbers, and started calling the people he had known in Indianapolis. He found, overall, three people that were still in the city. He had a lengthy conversation with each of them, telling them what was going on and asking for their help. All agreed to do whatever they could. One of them had been in Indianapolis for a long time and gave the impression he could rattle off the list of hospitals that was there in his younger days.

The Pastor began to feel better about the possibility of finding out more about Martin's history. He started to lay out his plans for resolving all this over the next few weeks. He was aware of a few places where Martin might get a job. He also knew of two or three church members, one of whom might provide a place for Martin to stay. Then he decided he needed to finish putting his sermon together for Sunday church services.

Over the next four days he was in continuous contact with his three friends in Indianapolis and trying to keep up with everything coming in to him. All of it together was starting to give him a good lead on where to get the answers he wanted. He also decided a good way to get information on Martin's first foster family was to contact the earliest one he remembered to see what they knew of the foster family that preceded them. He had gotten a few things on this family when he and Martin went to dinner and discussed his history.

Pastor Phil immediately started Googling the family name plus Indianapolis. The Indianapolis phonebook popped up on the screen showing the family's current address and phone number. He quickly dialed the number. When the phone was answered he introduced himself and told the entire story of his mission. They talked for forty-five minutes with Phil collecting all kinds of information including what he really needed, the name of the preceding foster family.

Now he took the next step, Googling the family whose name he had just learned. It took him three days to pin down where they lived. It turned out they had moved to Bloomington, Indiana. He only found them by Googling their last name plus Indiana, and then sorting through the list of names provided.

Pastor Phil called the number for this family. The phone was picked up on the second ring. He again explained his mission to the woman on the line. This turned out to be the mother in the family which had been the first foster family for Martin. She remembered Martin well, stating he had been a perfect baby, slept a lot, almost never cried, and loved to be held and talked to. They had to let him go to another foster home because her husband lost his job and they ran into money problems.

Finally, they got into a discussion about the hospital Martin had been born in and she did know the name of his mother. It turned out she also had a copy of his birth record which she had received from the hospital. He quickly asked if she would mail him a copy of the birth record. She said she would put it in the mail the next day.

Two days later, with the birth record in hand, he noted Marin's birth date listed as July, 1996 which made him seventeen years and seven months old. He only lacked five months to be able to register to vote. Phil immediately got in touch with the hospital, once again explained what he was doing, and started asking questions. The hospital was reluctant to release anything without the proper approval.

The Pastor called the first foster family back and asked if they could help get the hospital to approve releasing the information on Martin. They agreed to do so and said they were reasonably sure they could get the approval needed. Phil had Martin call the hospital and talk to them directly about the release. This two-pronged approach worked and three days later Phil had what he needed to try to trace

Martin's mother. From the birth certificate they knew her name was Elizabeth Joan Peters and now they had enough information for the final search to begin.

Several days later when Phil finally found some time he started the search again. This time he was searching for Martin's mother's name. After a while he had considerable data, most of it on her. Her birthplace was in Scottsburg, Indiana. She had lived in several towns in Indiana before settling in Bloomington where she met and married Jonathon Harry Peters. Further search on Jonathon Peters produced an obituary showing he passed away three years after Elizabeth. His obituary listed two brothers and two sisters. This gave Phil what he needed to do further searching. The obituary also listed names of Jonathon's parents, which, on further searching, Phil found had died in a car wreck two years ago. Their obituary listed the name of the funeral home so Phil decided to call them to see what he could obtain.

The next day, after a search for the phone number of the funeral home, Phil called them and talked to the Director. Again, explaining his purpose, he asked for the phone numbers and addresses of the listed surviving family members. Since Martin was a relative of the survivors, the Director had no qualms about meeting his request.. With this new information Phil proceeded to start contacting them. With the first call he struck pay dirt. Not only did this person, a brother to Martin's Father, remember Martin but also told Phil he should contact the law office of Duncan and Bornwell about Martin. It turned out this law office was handling the estate for Jack W. Peters who was Martin's paternal grandfather. Phil was told Jack Peters was in extremely poor health having had a series of heart attacks. He was expected to live only a matter of weeks. He was in the process of redoing his will and had been asking about Martin. Mr. Duncan told

Phil the estate was close to fifteen million dollars. Phil nearly fell off of his chair but regained enough composure to ask if part of the estate was going to go to Martin. Mr. Duncan replied, "That is absolutely Mr. Peters intent and now they could follow through since they had probably located Martin. The exact amount was not set yet, but he would be working with Mr. Peters to finalize everything."

He also said they would have to prove Martin was the true descendent before any final decisions could be made. Phil said he would supply everything he had dug up. He then contacted Martin to inform him he was seemingly seven months away from his goal of registering to vote but at this time he did not mention the money. Martin was elated to know this. He now knew when he could achieve his ambition of being a voter.

Copies of everything he had obtained on Martin was sent to Duncan and Bornwell. They spent a week checking everything out and finally decided everything was in order. They proceeded to notify Jack Peters of this. Jack finally decided he had all that he needed and directed his lawyers how he wanted his final last will set up. Martin was to receive two million dollars.

Jack passed away three weeks later and his will went into probate. An initial letter was sent to each of his heirs about the final resolution and how much money they would receive. Upon receipt of his letter Martin did three back flips in the aisle of the church and ran to tell Pastor Phil and to tell him the church would get four hundred thousand dollars for a new roof and new carpeting along with several other repairs the church badly needed. On hearing that the Pastor attempted a back flip, nearly breaking his arm before deciding just to be happy with what he had accomplished and the promised money for the church.

THE VISITOR

Harry Bascom was sitting at his desk going through bills when he suddenly felt as if somebody else was in the room. But he knew that couldn't be. He was the only one in the house. He looked around, saw nothing, and went back to shuffling his bills. With luck he would be able to pay all of them this month. Last month had been a bit of a nightmare concerning bills, but in the end he had managed to pay all of them. To do it he had skipped lunch for five days as well as not going out of the house for a week.

I need to get a part-time job, he thought. *At my age of seventy-one it won't be easy. Do they pay the greeters at the department store, I wonder? Something like that might help. I'll have to look into it.*

Just then he had that odd feeling again that he wasn't alone. *That's not possible*, he said to himself, *because I haven't had a visitor here for three months. I guess I'm just remembering how nice it was to have my Uncle visit me then, but he passed away a month ago.*

With that he went back to his bills. All of a sudden the feeling of having a visitor became stronger. He laid the bills down and started to get up, turning to his left as he did. Then he jumped up, knocking his chair over in the process. There sat his uncle on the sofa across the room. As he turned to run for the door he yelled in an excited, high pitched voice, "Who are you? How did you get in here? You look like my Uncle John. Who are you? Are you going to hurt me? Please don't hurt me." all of this said as he moved quickly towards the door.

The figure spoke up. "Don't be a ninny. Of course I'm your Uncle John. At least you had brains enough to recognize me. Now, sit down. We have to talk." In a sharper voice the figure said, "I told you to sit down. Do it now. We have to talk."

In his frightened state Harry couldn't move. "You have been dead for a month. I was at your funeral. I saw you in the casket. I saw you buried. You can't be here, you're dead."

"Are you going to babble on all night long or do you want to know why I'm here? I told you twice to sit down and I'm not going to do it again. SIT!"

Still frightened Harry quickly sat down and stared at the figure on his sofa. In taking a closer look he saw that the ghost was mostly transparent, but obviously his uncle. It was dressed in the clothes he was buried in. The same blue suit, red tie, and white shirt. Harry started to tremble a little bit again, but finally got himself under control.

"Excellent," the apparition said. "I'm glad you know to do what you're told. Now, we need to talk. I have some information for you. I know you're short of money and considering getting a part-time job. You really need the information I'm going to give you. I've told no one about a large stash of money I had hidden away. Something on the order of one hundred thousand dollars. I'm going to tell you where to find it. There is one condition you have to agree to. My daughter Janet, your first cousin in Peoria, has a problem and needs ten thousand dollars within three weeks to save her house. You will take care of that and the rest of the money is yours. Since you two are the only two heirs I have, you might consider doing more for her. Of course, as honest as you are you will report finding the money and paying the inheritance taxes. I'm sure you will agree to all of this. Further, since you are so honest, I suggest you consider splitting the money with her to help ease her future problems. Think about it."

Suddenly John started to fade out. Harry jumped up, saying, "You haven't yet told me where to find the money. I need more information or there is nothing I can do."

As the figure faded further it spoke one more time. "I will be back in three days. Then you will get all of the information you need. In the meantime, think about what I have told you."

The ghostly figure then disappeared completely. Harry sat back down, visibly shaking. Still not absolutely sure of what had just happened, his first thought was he had been having one of those vivid dreams he had had all his life. But this one seemed so real. He guessed he would know in three days.

The days passed quickly, with Harry switching easily from a state of anticipation to one of total fear and back again. He had no idea of what to actually expect. He hoped the ghost of his uncle would return and tell him where to find the money even though he feared he was hallucinating about talking to a ghost.

Finally the third day arrived and as Harry was having a beer and watching The Price is Right on television he heard a strange whiffing noise behind him. He slowly turned and saw his dead Uncle standing in the middle of the room.

He heard his Uncle's voice speak, eerily saying, "Well Harry, are you ready to continue?"

Harry's voice quavered a little as he responded, "Yes Sir. I am ready."

The ghost produced a piece of paper from somewhere. All Harry knew was suddenly the paper was there in the ghost's hand. The hand reached out towards Harry and indicated for him to take the paper. Harry slowly reached out and took hold of the edge of the paper farthest from where the ghost was holding it. The ghost let go and Harry stepped back three paces to open up a space between him and his Uncle. He turned the paper over, looked at it and pulled it closer to his eyes so he could study it. It was a map of someplace Harry did not recognize, but as he read the writing it became clearer. It turned out the map was of a place about two miles from where he lived. It was a wooded area at a local lake which drew a lot of fishermen and hikers. Harry realized that, if the money was buried there, it might be difficult to dig it up without being seen. As he studied the hand drawn map, drawn by whom he wondered, he realized the money was buried at the edge of the woods farthest from the lake and the walking path. This should make it easier to go in an hour before dusk and dig it up. He thought, "I wonder how deep it's buried. No more than two feet I hope."

Harry looked up just in time to see a semi-transparent hand waving goodbye. *I wonder if I'll ever see him again, he thought to himself. I still miss him greatly. He helped me many times when I needed it. I'll really try to do what he asked me to do.*

Harry decided to get started on the things he was asked to accomplish. First thing was to contact his cousin Janet and talk to her about what was happening without her deciding he was off his rocker. He picked up the phone and dialed her number. She picked up on the third ring saying, "Hello,

Harry. It's been a month since my father's funeral and I didn't get to talk to you very much then. What's up?"

Harry tried to keep his voice under control and said, "I've just gotten some information on a couple of things." He didn't want to go into any details of how he had obtained the information, so he jumped into what he had to say.

"Your father, my uncle, apparently left us a good chunk of money. Around fifty thousand dollars each." At that point Janet let out a small yell and asked, "How soon can I get it? I really need it."

"It will be about two weeks yet. I have to do some processing with government offices. I know a couple of people who can help me with that so I think I can speed things up. If I hit a snag I can get some money to you to protect your house. The main thing is I don't want either of us to get in deep trouble with the authorities."

Janet immediately asked, "How did you know about my house problem? I got the information on it only two weeks ago?"

Harry could only say, "It' a long story. I will tell you when this is finished."

Janet asked, "When are you going to dig it up?"

"I would rather not say yet. Not until I have actually found it where it's supposed to be. I'll let you know as soon as I know." was the response she got.

With that he said goodbye and went to collect his digging clothes and equipment. He was hoping the weather would hold as it was, just dreary enough to minimize walkers but not so bad he couldn't dig comfortably. He could only continue and see what happened.

Late in the afternoon Harry arrived at the park where the fishing pond was located. The first thing he did was to take a walk around to see if many people were there. There was a number of fishermen sitting around the edge of the lake. They were all concentrating on their fishing lines, and weren't going to move for some time to come. As he walked around the park some more he noticed there were almost no walkers or runners to be seen.

'Great,' he thought, 'maybe I can dig this evening.'

He proceeded to drive over to the area shown on the map his Uncle's ghost had given to him. He still shook a little at the thought of his Uncle's ghost, but he was slowly getting over it. He parked as close as he could to where he had to dig, hopped out of the car and took his shovel over to the exact spot. The map showed it to be exactly halfway between two big rocks. He looked around, saw no one, and started to dig. Fifteen minutes later his shovel hit something solid. He started shoveling more carefully and slowly uncovered a metal box about six inches square. He quickly lifted it out of the hole and without checking to see if it was locked, laid it to the side. He hurriedly started to refill the hole. In ten minutes he had finished. He went over and put the box in his car. Looking around he still saw no one. He hopped into his car and headed home. On the twenty minute drive home Harry continually muttered, "I hope. I hope. I hope."

Upon arriving at home he quickly grabbed the box and hurried indoors. he tried to open the box only to find that it was locked. "Now I have to find the key or a sledge hammer to break it open. "He finally guessed the key had been tied to the box and now was in the hole he had dug. He didn't want to risk going back and digging and sifting the dirt to find the key. He decided he would give a hammer a try. He took the box out into the garage, got his hammer, and started pounding on the lock. After the eighth hit the lock broke and he could force the box open. Inside he found, as he had hoped, two stacks of one hundred dollar bills.

After counting the money and noting it was exactly one hundred thousand dollars he called Janet and told her the good news. Janet asked again how he knew where the money was. Bill told her, "I got it in a package that was mailed to me. Apparently Uncle John had set up for it to be mailed to me after he found out he had a fatal disease."

They proceeded to discuss the procedures they had to go through. They knew they had to have proof the two of them were the only heirs. This part would be easy as Uncle John had left letters designating them as such. Next they had to report the find to the authorities knowing they could not say a ghost told them about it. They made up a story about John always talking about how in this economy you were better off just burying your money in the park. He also had talked about how he really loved the view in the park while sitting on a specific park bench and that he had spent hours there relaxing. Harry remembered that there was a park bench about ten feet away from where he had dug. He had the letter in which John gave a specific location very close to that bench mentioning that there was something important to him there. Everyone had just assumed it was the view.

The next step was to process all of this through the authorities in order to completely clear the air. With the evidence they actually had plus the details they had made up Harry and Janet had no problem clearing the authorities hurdle. There were a couple of tough questions about the authenticity of some of the pieces of paper. Harry managed to answer those to everyone's satisfaction.

Finally they had everything registered properly with the two of them listed as the heirs. They finally headed to their banks to deposit the money. Before they parted they decided to get together the next week to discuss what each one of them was going to do with the money. Harry headed back home to write checks for his bills. For once he could pay all of them on time.

As Harry sat at his desk, he could swear he heard a voice laughing just like his Uncle John used to do. He looked around and could see nothing. He guessed his Uncle laughed because he had achieved his goal and would not need to reappear.

THE BROTHERS

Two young men in the yard raked leaves and prepared to mow the lawn. They were acting as if they had other things on their mind. They also seemed to greatly resemble each other. One turned to the other, "You know, Ron, you sorta look like me. Have we met before? Could we possibly be related?"

"Don, you're a dummy. Of course you look like me. You're my identical twin brother. Now shut up and get started on these leaves so we can mow the lawn."

"I really enjoy pulling your leg. You always fall for it."

"I'll pull your leg off and put it where it doesn't belong. Now get to work. We have to finish Mom's lawn so I can go back home and do some of my work. My wife has a whole list of jobs waiting for me."

"Careful, Ron. Your sense of humor is slipping."

"I'm not worried. She's soundly napping on the sofa, and I know you won't disturb her right now."

"You keep up this BS and I'll have no qualms about waking her."

"Say, Ron, can you tell me why 'slow down' and 'slow up' mean the same thing?"

"Well if you don't know that, you probably don't understand why 'fat chance' and 'slim chance' mean the same thing."

"Why don't we go to the library and look up those things?"

"Let's just Google it, Don. We have a better chance of finding the answer."

"Well, while we're at it, we can look up why 'wise man' and 'wise guy' are opposites, as well as why 'over look' and 'over see' are opposites."

"I thought we were going to get to work," Ron said, "I won't start before you do."

"I'm starting. I'm starting. I only have an hour left before I have to head home. If I'm not there on time my wife will give me holy heck. She has plans for this evening.

"Well, my wife has plans also. It involves eating supper and making sure we see Big Bang Theory at 8:00 pm."

They finally dove into the waiting work. After finishing the leaf raking, they got the mowers they had brought and started on the lawn with big smiles on each of their faces. As they went back and forth, passing each other many times, they used each passing as a chance to continue with the puns and jokes.

On the first passing Don spoke loudly, "Did you know a backward poet writes inverse."

Ron immediately responded, "I heard about that, but did you know a chicken crossing the road is poultry in motion."

As they approached each other for the second time, Ron spoke, "I understand that in a democracy your vote counts. In feudalism it's your Count that votes.

'Well did you know about the Local Area Network in Australia," Don retorted. It's called the LAN down under."

On the third passing, the following exchange occurred, "Hey, I heard about a short fortune-teller who escaped from prison. She was a small medium at large."

Donald J. Peacock

"Yeah, but you have to remember, if you don't pay your exorcist, you can get repossessed."

As the fourth passing approached, both Ron and Don were trying to look away and to keep from breaking out in laughter. Just as they passed Ron broke into laughter and said, "I was at the baseball game the other day and I wondered why the baseball kept getting bigger. Then it hit me."

Don joined in the laughter. "No matter how much you push the envelope, it'll still be stationary."

By the fifth passing they were really trying hard to outdo each other. Don called out, "Two antennas met on a roof, fell in love and got married. The ceremony wasn't much, but the reception was excellent."

Ron had a weak response. "A gossip is someone with a great sense of rumor." Then he shouted. "I win that one."

"We'll see about that," Ron replied.

After finishing half of the mowing they took and a quick break and sat and drank some water. Don commented, "I know a story you don't. A group of chess enthusiasts checked into a hotel and were standing in the lobby discussing their recent tournament victories. After about an hour, the manager came out of the office and asked them to disperse. 'But why,' they asked, as they moved off. 'Because', he said, 'I can't stand chess-nuts boasting in an open foyer.'" Both laughed.

"Well, here's one you probably haven't heard, "Ron said. 'A woman has twins and gives them up for adoption. One of them goes to a family in Egypt and is named "Ahmal." The other goes to a family in Spain; they named him "Juan." Years later, Juan sends a picture of himself to his birth mother. Upon receiving the picture, she tells her husband that she wishes she also had a picture of Ahmal. Her husband responds, "They're identical twins. If you've seen Juan, you've seen Ahmal.'"

At that point they decided that they needed to finish the lawn, so they started their mowers and went back to work.

At the sixth passing they both thought the game was over and almost went by each other without saying anything. Suddenly Ron said, "I used to work in a blanket factory, but it folded."

"That's nothing." Don responded, I used to know a man who fell into an upholstery machine. He's now fully recovered."

On the seventh passing, Don called out, "I'm going to get a little kinky, and I bet you don't have an answer. I think Politicians and diapers should be changed often. For the same reason."

Ron instantly responded, "A hole has been found in the nudist camp wall. The police are looking into it."

The eighth time they were farther apart and had to call out fairly loudly, but they were capable of it. Ron got in first, "Did you hear that a rubber band pistol was confiscated from algebra class, because it was a weapon of math disruption."

"Well, speaking of scholarly things, were you aware that a book on voyeurism is a peeping tom?"

The ninth time, close to finishing the yard, Don spoke first. "Did you hear about the dog that gave birth to puppies near the road and was cited for littering."

"No, I didn't but I bet you didn't know that a successful diet is the triumph of mind over platter."

As they crossed for the tenth time, to finish the mowing, Don spoke first, "I heard you have a photographic memory that was never developed."

"Well", Ron responded, "I heard that you tried for a job as a gold miner, but it didn't pan out."

As they finished and rolled their mowers over to their cars to put them in the trunks, Mom came out the front door, "I heard all of those bad jokes. Since you have already disturbed all of the neighbors, I'll have to join in and tell some blonde jokes. My first one is 'There was a blonde, a brunette, and a redhead. They had a magic mirror. If you told the truth you got rich. If you told a lie, you disappeared. The brunette said, "I'm the smartest girl in the world." POOF! The redhead said, "I'm the prettiest girl in the world." POOF! The blonde said, "I think..." POOF!"

"Wait, I have a second one, 'There was a blonde who had two horses and couldn't tell them apart. She decided to cut part of one's tail off, but it grew back. She then shaved part of the horse's ear, but it grew back. She gave up and just decided to keep the white horse in one barn and the black one in another."

"And finally, before you two go home to your families, one final one liner. 'What are the worst three years of a blonde's life? Third grade."

That's all the jokes I can remember right now. If I think of any more I'll e-mail you. Thank both of you for doing my lawn again. I'll have to have both of you and your families over for dinner real soon."

- All puns, jokes, etc. used in this story came from various internet websites.

THE VALENTINE'S DAY CARDS

Jennifer sat at her desk at work finishing a project due that day. Even as she worked, she kept an eye on the clock. She had two hours to finish the project. She was very excited about getting home. It was the fourteenth of February and a very important piece of mail would be in her mail box.

Every year, for the last five years, she had received a Valentine's Day card, and it had become very important to her. The card was always anonymous but it always had a beautiful message for her.. She knew it came from somebody who loved her very much. She was thirty-two years old and had never been married. She yearned to have a child. She knew she would be a great mother the same as her mother had been.

Finally, she wrapped up her project, turned it in, and left work for home. Arriving home she checked her mailbox and among the mail was the Valentine card in a pink envelope, She tore it open and it was the card she was expecting. She also noted this year it contained a short poem:

Roses are Red,
Violets are Blue,
You are Beautiful,
And Live Close to Me.

Jennifer loved the poem and read it again aloud. A tear started down one cheek. She checked the card to see if there was anything to identify the sender, but, as usual, there was no way to tell. This year, at least, the poem said it was from somebody who lived nearby.

She mentally ran through the people living on her block but she couldn't think of anyone who would be sending her Valentine Cards. She tried to think of those living within three blocks of her, but wasn't familiar enough with all of them.

She decided to talk to the Johnsons, who lived three houses away. She had become good friends with them and she and Alice Johnson shared many things. She hoped Alice could help her figure out who might be sending the cards.

She walked to the Johnson's house and was invited in.

"Alice, can you think of anyone locally who might be sending me valentine cards."

"I'll have to think about it for a bit because no one comes immediately to mind."

The front door swung open and Bill Johnson walked in followed closely by Harold, the twelve year old foster child the Johnsons had taken in seven years before. Bill went over and gave Jennifer a great big hug.

"Jennifer, what brings you over?"

"I needed to talk to Alice about some things."

"Well, it's always great to see you." He then headed to the back room to finish some things on the computer.

Harold went over to Jennifer to say hello. He did so in a very bashful manner, but grinned real big when Jennifer gave him a hug. Then he quickly turned and hurried to the back room where Bill had gone.

After Harold left Alice turned to Jennifer and asked, "Can I discuss something with you?". At a 'yes, certainly' she started to explain, "There is an upcoming problem for

Bill and I that will preclude our staying on as foster parents to Harold. Bill is being transferred to Britain for his job and I will be going with him, obviously." Then she started to softly cry.

"I hate to hear that," said Jennifer. "He's such a nice young boy. What's going to happen to him?"

"I don't know. He'll have to go back into the Foster Child Bureau of the Child Protective System. It'll destroy him. This has been the only real home he has ever known."

"That would be terrible. What's the possibility of my becoming his foster parent? He would be with someone he knows and be able to stay in the same neighborhood and go to the same school."

"Let's call the Child Fostering Service and talk to them," Alice suggested. "That would be a great solution if they allow it. Your being single might be the only problem I can think of, but since Harold is in school from eight-thirty in the morning to three-thirty in the afternoon plus a half hour getting home on the bus it might not be considered a big problem. Do you think you could be home each day by four o'clock?"

"I'm pretty sure I could work it out with my boss. During the summer I could use one of the day-care services. Alice, why don't you call the Foster Service and talk to them about it. The fact Harold knows me and we get along great should be a big help. I'll be at home. Call me and let me know what they say."

Two hours later Alice called Jennifer and relayed the good news. The Foster Service people wanted to talk to her as soon as possible about Harold.

The next morning Alice called the Foster Service and they set up an appointment for herself and Jennifer to talk to them three days later. Jennifer was excited about the possibility of fostering Harold. She was told not to say anything to Harold until after the meeting.

On the following Thursday Jennifer and Alice showed up at the Foster Service office. Alice was prepared to fully support Jennifer. She knew most of the people in the office quite well.

They were ushered into George Kantell's office and sat down across from his desk. He was not there yet, but showed up ten minutes later. He took his chair and they spent an hour discussing all of the points around Jennifer becoming Harold's foster parent. Almost everything supported the action.

As Jennifer talked about herself and all of the pros and cons she couldn't help noticing that George seemed young for the responsibilities of his job. Actually she thought he was about her age. She couldn't help noticing that he seemed intelligent and he was good looking.

As they finished up, George said, "I need to be getting home."

"Your wife preparing dinner?" Jennifer asked?

"No. I'm not married. I have two cats and a dog that will need food and a walk."

Jennifer felt her heart rise. "I'll have some free time Friday afternoon. Maybe we can continue this talk and resolve any remaining problems."

"That would be fine," George replied. "Meet here at three-thirty?"

"That would be ideal. I'll be here at that time."

Friday came quickly and Jennifer walked into George's office promptly at three-thirty. George jumped up and greeted her warmly, thinking, *She is a very attractive woman. Maybe I can invite her out sometime.*

They talked till five o'clock, not always about fostering a child. They drifted into several personal discussions with both of them obviously enjoying it.

The final result of the two meetings was George recommended Jennifer be appointed Harold's foster parent. His bosses reviewed George's recommendations on the matter, and in the end agreed with him. George said he would relay the information to Jennifer.

He called Jennifer and told her he wanted to drop by and update her on the decision his office had reached.

"I was just starting to fix supper," She said. "There is enough for two, so plan on eating here."

"Yes. I can do that," George responded. I'll head over in ten minutes. I have to clear my desk."

Twenty minutes later, George pulled into Jennifer's driveway and commented, "Thank goodness for GPS units." He went to the front door, rang the doorbell and was quickly invited in. He noted some great smells coming out of the kitchen. "She must be a good cook."

Jennifer invited him into the living room and offered him a small glass of wine. They sat and talked for a few minutes while things in the kitchen finished up. George's offer to help carry things into the dining room was quickly accepted. At last they sat down and started filling their plates. "Boy, if I ate like this every night I would really put on weight," he observed.

"You can take smaller portions you know," Jennifer said.

"This stuff is too good to take smaller portions," George said. "I'll have to hit the gym tomorrow night."

As they ate, they indulged in chit chat. After eating and clearing off the table, they went into the living room to talk about Harold. As soon as he said his office had approved her as acceptable as Harold's foster parent, she jumped up, ran over, and gave him a great big hug.

He suppressed the feeling he should give her a kiss, but only for a moment. He leaned over and kissed her on the cheek. She turned more towards him and he kissed her on the lips. A short, gentle kiss. As they parted and started to sit back down, George said, "I really do need to get home and take care of my animals. Do you think we might go out for dinner and a show some Saturday evening."

"I would love to do that. This Saturday is fine with me."

"OK, then we'll do that. I'll pick you up at five-thirty if that's OK."

"That's fine. I'll see you then."

The next morning Jennifer went over to the Johnsons to tell them the good news. She spoke with Alice and Bill, reviewing what had happened at the second meeting with George and at her house over dinner. At the mention of dinner at Jennifer's house, Alice's eyes widened and a grin appeared on her face which she tried unsuccessfully to stifle.

Then they called Harold in to tell him the good news. He listened all the way through and then ran over and gave Jennifer a big hug and a kiss on the cheek.

"That's great. I'll be a very good boy for you.

Roses are red,

Violets are blue,

You are beautiful,

And live close to me."

Jennifer's eyes got wide with an astonished look on her face. "Where did you hear that poem?"

"I wrote it," he said.

"But that was on a Valentine card I got yesterday. Who sent it?"

"I sent you the card," he mumbled and blushed.

Jennifer had an even more astonished look on her face. "Are you the one who has been sending me a valentine's card for the last five years?"

"Yes, I sent those," he said as he glanced at the floor and shuffled his feet

At that point Alice jumped in. "I think I understand what's happened. For six years Harold and his classmates have been exchanging Valentine cards. I buy a bunch for him, and he writes in them and addresses each one with a classmate's name. Apparently, he has been sending you one of those cards without my knowing it. Is that true, Harold?"

"Yes. I think Jennifer is a really nice lady, and I enjoyed sending her a card each year."

"Well, I enjoyed getting them. I think I may have gotten three Valentine's Day gifts this year - Harold's card, meeting George and fostering Harold."

Santa to the Rescue

"**M**ary, honey, the doctor has reassured me it is not a major problem."

"Jim, that's what they told Janet."

"Yes, but her cancer was much more advanced than yours, and it had spread to several organs. Dr. Blake said all of the tests are indicating yours has been discovered very early and apparently has not spread at all."

"I felt there was a lot of iffiness in those reports. Dr. Blake, when he talked to me, seemed to have a lot of hesitation in his voice. He said he wanted to schedule my surgery as soon as possible, and this turns out to be three days before Christmas. That's the part I'm really worried about this whole thing leaving you with five kids to raise by yourself. It would certainly leave you, at a minimum, having to make sure the kids have a good Christmas."

"I know. It all worries me also, but I'm assuming all will go well and I can handle it while you recuperate. Don't let those kinds of worries occupy your thoughts. Just keep your mind on all things going well and have a quick recovery."

"Dr. Blake said if all things go well I should be in the hospital until mid-January and then I would be released with just a few limitations. He said those limitations include cleaning, lifting things. He said I should plan on getting lots of rest. He said he could include cooking as a limitation if I wanted."

"I'll have to talk to him about that list," Jim said, starting to smile. "At least we have one present bought for each of the kids. Not enough, but some."

Three days before Christmas Jim's sister came to the house to stay with the kids while Jim drove Mary to the hospital. He planned on staying there until she came out of surgery and staying long enough to know she was all right.

Two and a half hours later Mary came out of surgery and was taken directly to a recovery room. Jim then had a chance for a short discussion with the surgeon who told him everything had gone extremely well. The cancer had not had a chance to spread. The surgeon said, "I am sure I got all of the cancer and Mary will live a long and happy life. Of course the happy part is pretty well up to you. She will be in the hospital for two weeks and then she can go home. At home she is still to get plenty of rest and not lift anything heavier than two pounds for three months. Even after three months she has to be careful for a bit longer, something like four months longer. After that she should be good to go."

Jim thanked the surgeon and went into Mary's room to await her recovery from the anesthetics, which, as it turned out, took four hours. As Mary started to stir around Jim moved over next to the bed so he would be the first thing she saw. As she stirred further and started looking around she spotted Jim and a grin appeared on her face.

"I must have survived the surgery if you are there looking so happy."

"Yes, you not only survived the surgery, your surgeon said you should live a long and happy life, but he stressed I'm responsible for the happy part."

"That shouldn't be too hard. I'm so happy just to see you."

An hour later as Mary went back to sleep, Jim headed home to help his sister with the kids. On the way home he was trying to think of a way to make this Christmas better for his kids since Mary would still be in the hospital. Then a thought popped into his mind. Get someone to play Santa on Christmas Eve. The question was who. He decided it was top priority over the next day and a half.

As he pulled into his driveway, he saw his new neighbor, Mark, out in front of his house. Jim quickly pulled to a stop, exclaiming, "He's somewhat overweight, he would make a perfect Santa. I Hope I can talk him into it. From what I have seen he would make a perfect 'Jolly Santa Claus'."

With the idea in his mind, Jim headed over to Mark to gently raise the topic with him. Mark saw him coming, so he laid down his clippers and held out his hand.

"Hi Jim, How are you doing today?"

"I'm doing as well as can be expected. My wife is in the hospital and will be there till mid-January."

"I'm sorry to hear that, Jim. What's the problem?"

"She has cancer, but the surgeon is certain he got all of it. We just need to stay up-beat and get things done until she comes home."

"Is there anything I can do to help, Jim."

"Well, Mark, since you ask. We need to have Christmas for our five kids. I've bought a few gifts for them, and I haven't had a chance to get any more. Those few will have to do this year. My real question is this, is there any way I can talk you into playing Santa on Christmas Eve. Our kids don't really know you, so they shouldn't recognize your voice."

"I would be glad to play Santa for all of you. I think you are a really nice family and great neighbors. My first question is where do I get a Santa outfit?"

"I think I can take care of that problem. This morning I saw a shop having a sign in the window saying 'Santa Outfits Still Available'. If you're not busy in the morning, maybe we could fix you up with one of theirs."

"OK. Tomorrow morning is fine. About 9 am."

"Mark, I can pay you to do this for us. Name your amount."

"Jim, why don't you just donate the money to your favorite charity. Now I really need to finish trimming these bushes. See you in the morning."

The next day Jim and Mark headed out to see if they could rent an outfit for Mark. It turned out they found one fitting Mark perfectly. They rented it along with a big white beard. They also found a set of red gloves to go with the outfit.

As they headed home, Jim explained they had only had time to get one present for each of the kids, but they were presents the kids really wanted.

Mark's response was, "I guess we will just have to do our best. We really don't have any other choice."

At 6pm on Christmas Eve, there came a knock on the front door. Jim opened the door, and there stood Santa with a bag of presents. Jim invited him in and called loudly for the kids to come see who is here, all the while trying to act surprised. The kids came running into the room, see Santa and start jumping for joy. As Santa entered Jim said, "Welcome. Welcome. Come in. The kids are obviously glad to see you. I see you have your bag of toys. I hope some of them are for my kids."

Santa said, in a deep voice, "Ho. Ho. Ho. Merry Christmas. Yes, I have presents for the kids."

The kids were still bouncing up and down and yelling, "Santa is here. Santa is here. What did you bring us?"

The two older kids joined in to encourage the three younger ones, even though they strongly felt Santa didn't really exist. They did know there would be presents for them also.

Santa opened up his bag and started pulling out gifts, looking at the name on it, and handing it to the child whose name he saw. As he went through the presents, with each child getting three or four, he had no hesitation in knowing which child was to receive it.

Jim kept thinking, "Mark doesn't know any of my kids, how can he be so accurate in distributing these things? There are some very strange things going on here."

When Santa had handed out the last gift, seventeen in all, Jim's amazement grew by leaps and bounds.

Finally Santa said, "All of you have a very merry Christmas, go see your mother in the hospital, and be good for the coming year."

The second oldest child, George, said, "We visited her earlier today and dad's going to take us back to see her this evening."

As Santa exited out the door he said, "I think your Aunt Jean is doing a superb job taking care of you kids and helping your father out in this his time of need. Merry Christmas and Happy New Year."

Then he handed Jim a sealed envelope saying, "Open this tomorrow. Good night all."

After Santa had left Jim called Mary and each of the kids talked to her, each of them saying, "They wished she had been home for Santa's visit and to see the gifts they received."

Jim told her all about Santa and how he had provided all of the gifts the kids wanted.

Mary asked, "How did Santa know what all presents the kids wanted?"

Jim couldn't give her an answer. He had told her about the new neighbor playing Santa, but he had never told him what presents the kids wanted.

The kids all took turns talking to their mom about Santa, until mom had to get some sleep. All of the kids said they were looking forward to seeing her tomorrow.

The next morning, after Jim had helped his sister fix breakfast for everybody, he took time to open the envelope Santa had given him. It contained a short note saying, 'Don't worry. They found all of Mary's cancer and removed it. She'll live a long and happy life'.

Jim really began to wonder how his neighbor, a mechanical engineer, knew so much about his family.

Jim rounded up all the kids and took them to the hospital to visit their mother. While there, he got a chance to talk to the surgeon again. The surgeon said, "From all of the after-surgery tests, I'm quite certain we got all of the cancer. They would have to keep an eye on things for, probably, several years, with regular checkups".

When Jim and the kids got home he went over to see his neighbor, who immediately started to apologize, saying he is sorry he couldn't accomplish the playing of Santa. He said, "I was extremely sick Christmas Eve and couldn't even get out of bed, let alone play Santa, or pick up a phone and call you. I was near comatose Christmas Eve and most of this morning. I don't think I have ever felt so bad at any time in my life."

Jim started to stammer, saying, "But Santa was at our house. How did you get someone to play Santa. How did he get the gifts the kids wanted and how did he know Mary would be fine?"

Mark could only reply, "I have no idea."

Jim started to think, Maybe Santa Claus is real.

HE'S COMING

That time of the year was approaching rapidly again. It seems like it just ended for last year. I have already started to sweat excessively and have also begun having trouble sleeping. I don't know if I can get through this another time. I have started to look through the phone book for a psychologist. I don't know if I can afford one but I may not have a choice. This fear started when I was six years old. I am now fifty-two. Forty-six years is a long time to bear the fear I have. I must find a way to overcome it.

Let me start at the beginning. When I was little I always jumped for joy when they said Santa Claus was coming. I knew he always brought a lot of nice gifts which I enjoyed a great deal. But I was also told if I wasn't good Santa wouldn't bring me any presents and he might do something to punish me. And the year I was six, terrible things happened. On Christmas day I woke up early and rushed out to the living room where the Christmas tree was set up. I saw there were no presents under the tree. As I approached the tree I also saw the food we always set out for Santa was gone. The plates were totally empty. Then I saw there was a small flame burning behind the tree. Dad always set a small lit candle beside the food so Santa could find it easier. Santa must have knocked it over. I ran back to my room, terrified. I didn't know what to do. Then I heard my parents getting up.

They came out to the living room, saw the fire, and started yelling, "Call the Fire Department. I think Santa started a fire after he got done eating."

They were bustling all over the place with Mom calling the Fire Department and Dad trying to put out the fire. By the time the fire truck arrived the tree was almost burned through and the wall was black from flame and smoke. I stayed in my room during all of this.

It took an hour to put out the flame and get things cooled down and it was two days before everything was cleaned up. All during this process Dad and Mom continuously talked about Santa destroying Christmas for us. No presents and Santa tried to burn the house down. That was Christmas when I was six.

It has left me terrified of Christmas time. I realize all kids really look forward to that time of year but they have never experienced anything like I have. My hands start to shake just thinking about it. I still feel I must stay awake in late December in case Santa produces another disaster. I feel he might even come early and do so. I must stay awake and be prepared to battle it. I still send a message every year to Santa at the North Pole telling him not to come to my house. I don't think he ever gets the message. It's like he totally doesn't understand.

Twenty years ago I met a beautiful woman, a widow, who had two small children six and seven years old. We were married eighteen years ago. She is a wonderful woman and the delight of my life. The problem has been she always wanted me to play Santa at Christmas time for her two children and later for her grandchildren. When she does I always start to shake. One year I even started to cry with fear.

People try to tell me the reason I received no presents that year was probably because my parents returned all of them in order to get money to repair the damage done by the fire. They also claim Dad probably knocked the candle over when he got the food.

I can't trust those people. They weren't there. They don't know what happened. I was there. It was and still is the most frightening thing that ever happened to me. I will never get over it.

MY BIG WHITE CAT

On December 20, 2010 I lost one of my best friends. As he lay on the vet's table being checked I reached out to touch his tail. He jerked his head around and nipped my hand. I truly realized at that point what great pain and agony he was in.

His given name was Buzz Newman Stubby Fluffalump Jaws. The name Buzz came from the fact that he buzzed loudly when we picked him up, Newman because he had Paul Newman blue eyes, Stubby because of his short legs, Fluffalump because he was a fluffy lump, and Jaws because he would bite if he got really peeved. He wound up just being called Newman.

We already had three cats. The oldest was a black and white tuxedo female named Chelsea we got from a 'friend'. The next oldest was a female orange tiger named Weesie I found running loose with her mother in DeWeese park. They had obviously been abandoned. The mother cat ran away when I approached them and was not to be caught. The kitten came running to me. She promptly had a new home.

As I drove home, she settled down on my lap and lay there for the rest of the ride. Our youngest cat was a male orange tiger named Tucker we found as a kitten walking in the gutter on Xenia Avenue. We stopped and my wife hopped out of the van and went over to get him as a police car waited behind us while we picked him up. Tucker was completely congested from an infection. His eyes were totally closed with pus. He was probably less than ten minutes from being road kill. We took him straight to the vet; five days and $300 later we had our third cat.   One day in July, 2004 we went to lunch and afterwards we stopped in a pet store for some supplies for our three cats and wound up buying a fourth cat, Newman. He had no hair on his tummy and no hair on his neck. His ID tag was wrapped tightly around his neck and it had rubbed off a band of hair. His eyes looked at me saying you need another cat. For $199 plus tax he was our cat. We probably didn't need another cat but how could anyone pass up those eyes.

His official listing was "Date of Birth 5/14/04, type of cat - male Persian cat, Unregisterable". He was actually probably a mixed Persian and Himalayan.

After we got him home and cut his neck tag off, he settled in with the other cats and they readily accepted him. He did eventually grow hair on his tummy and his neck and started to put on some weight. He also started to demonstrate some strange characteristics, but more on that later.

He quickly turned into my cat, initially because I was the one who fed him. But then it went way past feeding.

Being a white long haired cat, we started finding white hair on everything in the house; sofas, chairs, clothes, bed linens, everything. We tried to comb him often but as we would work on his numerous hair mats he would finally get tired of it and then you had better be fast or you would have bite marks on your hands. We did the best we could.

As he got more attached to me, he started doings things like getting between my feet any time I stood up. He then stuck his rear end up in the air waiting to get his back scratched. He followed me around like a little puppy would. At night he would hop into bed beside me and snuggle tightly up against my leg. If I rolled over he would wait and then move back against my leg.

As soon as I hopped out of bed in the morning, he was right there underfoot, saying in cat actions, "Good morning. Are we going to have breakfast?" When my wife and I were out someplace and came home, he would rush to the door as soon as we entered to greet us. He wanted me to talk to him. I couldn't go anywhere in the house without him following me.

The strangest characteristic referred to above was as he got older he developed the weirdly unique habit of eating paper. It wasn't something he did once in a while, it was anytime he heard paper crumple, crinkle or tear he was right there.

He particularly loved things like the waxed paper stamps came on. This reached the point that whenever he heard the desk drawer pulled open he came running because he knew we were probably getting a stamp. While I peeled off a stamp there was a little white cat under foot with his blue eyes staring up at the sheet of stamps waiting for me to give him a small piece. I relented and gave him some every once in a while. My mistake. It only encouraged him.

It finally reached the point where a noise of any kind of paper brought him running and begging. It turned out the eating of paper was probably the first indication of problems to come. The real indication of a problem came in early May, 2006. We noticed that Newman was going continuously to his potty pan and trying to urinate with very little success. He was also excessively licking his rear end. On May 14, 2006 we took him to the vet. They held him overnight and emptied his bladder but couldn't really find anything wrong with him.. We brought him home the next day and he ran out of the carrier into the house. He did not like the vet. Everything seemed to be back to normal, including the excessive desire for paper.

His second visit to the vet was on January 22, 2008 for the same problem; urination difficulties. We had been trying not to leave any kind of paper out overnight. If we slipped up he would invariably find it and eat a small chunk.

His third visit to the vet was on June 16, 2009. Same problem, same temporary solution. We had become extremely diligent about the paper problem, but somehow, every so often, he would find something that we had thought was safe from him. Our house was becoming much cleaner. He did have that effect on us.

The fourth visit to the vet was on October 25, 2010. Again same problem, same solution. After each visit he would seem to do all right for about a year to a year and a quarter, then the problem would show up and get very intense for the little fellow. The eating of the paper was never the cause of the problem, it was the most distinct indication of the problem.

His bladder and urinary tract were slowly (maybe quickly) degenerating with only temporary recovery and the recovery each time not as much. Degeneration, degeneration, degeneration.

Not quite two months after his fourth visit the problem reoccurred with more intensity. Back to the vet. He urinated in his carrier on the way. At the vets he was urine soaked and bloody. The vet kept him overnight and then called us. He talked to my wife because I knew what needed to be done and I couldn't say it. After a short discussion with my wife, she told the vet of our final decision. Euthanization. No other option existed. We all understood it at that point. My wife asked the vet if, after putting him down, they would see that his body went to The Narrows, an animal cemetery.

On 20 December, 2010 he was put down. He was scared, sick and in great pain. We had briefly discussed urinary tract surgery with the vet. This would have involved totally rebuilding the urinary tract with a subsequent long recuperation and no certainty that it would solve the problem. It would have been pure Hell for him. He was way too nice a cat to put him through that.

His life was shorter, much shorter, than any other cat we ever had, but he had brought so much into our lives, particularly mine.

The next day, after Newman's euthanization, Tucker, our other male cat, twice circled our bed where Newman usually slept. He was searching for Newman. He missed his friend also.

Newman was my cat.

More than that he was my friend.

Much more than that I miss him.

I will always miss him.

For the rest of my life.

EATING OUT

"Pete, you have to remember, I'm on curfew. If I'm not home by 10:00 pm, my parents will ground me for a month."

"Linda, I remember your curfew, but I figure that now you're eighteen so curfew doesn't count any more. Besides, it's the twenty-ninth, so if you're grounded for the month that's only two days. I'll wait for you."

"You idiot. It's for *a* month not *the* month. But I think it's still all right since my neighbors have a really good looking son. Plus he owns a better car than you do. It probably doesn't stall out when you really need it."

Pete tried to make a joke and said, "Mine doesn't stall out very often. Just once per date. It's really worked great for me many times."

"I think I'll slap you up the side of the head."

Pete responded, "It wouldn't bother anything if you did. I played football all through high school. I have so many concussions your hit would be soft enough to be healing."

Linda returned, "Then maybe I'll get a piece of wood over there and use it. That should make a difference."

"I should know not to get smart with you. You're too intelligent for me to do that."

"Keep it in mind in the future."

Pete tried to change the subject, saying, "I'll work on it. A new restaurant has opened up by Johnson Park. Would you like to get something to eat?"

"Sounds good. I hope they have good hamburgers. Plus, maybe they'll have some good pie for dessert."

"That's all it takes for you to give a restaurant a five star rating, isn't it?"

Linda said with a bit of exasperation, "Well, all it takes for you to do the same is a good bowl of soup and a chicken salad sandwich. Let's get going. I'm getting hungry."

"Hop in the car and we're off."

It was a twenty minute drive to the Johnson Park area, followed by almost ten minutes of searching for the new restaurant. Finally they found it and as they pulled into the parking lot, they noticed the lot was surrounded on three sides by seven foot tall bushes. That struck them as strange, but at this time their primary thoughts were on eating.

Entering the restaurant, Pete commented, "It's strange they would have those tall bushes right there at the edges of the parking lot. It seems it would create a lot of extra work cleaning up the leaves."

"It would, and they're tall enough and thick enough for somebody to hide behind them so they could rob patrons as they were heading in or out of the restaurant", replied Linda.

Once inside they were quickly seated and started looking through the menu.

"They have hamburgers. The picture makes them look really good. Oh Pete, they have peach pie. My favorite. I think I'm going to like this place."

"I see they have tomato basil soup, my favorite. But they don't have a chicken salad sandwich, so I guess I'll have to settle for a hamburger also."

The waitress, whom Pete noted looked great in her mini-skirt, got their orders and went to the computer to input them.

Linda said, "I saw you looking at her legs."

"Yes, I'm guilty. They are almost as nice as yours."

"Good recovery. Now when she brings the food you can look at me."

Pete settled a little deeper in his chair and said, "Yes Ma'am."

Finally, their food arrived and they dove into it. Both were unusually hungry. Plus, as promised, Pete didn't look at the waitress's legs, or at least, tried to pretend he didn't. Linda was somewhat impressed he had made the effort, even though he wasn't one hundred percent successful. She gave him credit for trying.

As they ate they continued to discuss the tall bushes around the parking lot. To them it seemed senseless to have them.

Linda said, "I saw on the news earlier a monkey has escaped from the zoo about four blocks from here. I wonder if it could be in those bushes. It's probably hungry by now."

They finished eating and Linda went to the ladies room while Pete paid the bill. He over-tipped the waitress by two dollars because she had such good looking legs. He went to the lobby to wait for Linda so she wouldn't know about it.

When Linda joined him in the lobby, the first thing she said was, "How much did you over-tip?"

"I don't get away with anything with you, do I?"

"I told you earlier, I know you pretty well by now, so there isn't much you can get away with."

"I'll try to keep that in mind in the future.

"Good luck," was the response he got from Linda as she tried not to laugh too loudly. "Also, remember I have to be home in one hour."

They started out to the parking lot. As they walked towards their car, Pete noticed the tall bushes moving like there was a strong wind blowing. He looked up towards the American flag in front of the building, noticing it was hanging straight down, indicating no wind at all. He started looking closely at the bushes, seeing only two or three of them shaking.

When they neared the car the bushes started shaking much harder. All of a sudden two figures stepped through the bushes and walked into the parking lot, their arms extended out ahead of them.

Pete took one look and yelled, "Those are zombies. I didn't think they actually existed!"

"What's a zombie? I don't understand. Are we in trouble?"

"If we don't get in the car immediately we are in deep trouble. Zombies kill people for the fun of it."

"I hope you're kidding, but just in case unlock the car. NOW!!"

Pete pulled his key ring out of his pocket and punched the door unlock button. "Run for the car. Get in. Hurry. I don't know of anything a zombie fears. They have no nerves, no known fears, and no mercy for anything."

Pete and Linda jumped into their car. Pete hit the door-lock button just as the zombies reached the front fender of the car. The zombies stood there waving their arms. Pete started to think he would have to risk running over them to get away.

Suddenly, one of the zombies turned to his right, took one look, and started wildly reacting to what he saw. He was waving his arms, shaking his head, and hitting the second zombie on the head and shoulders.

The second zombie turned to the right and started reacting as wildly as the first zombie had. The two of them turned around and started fleeing back towards the bushes. They were trying to move so fast they staggered and almost fell.

Pete and Linda looked around to see what was going on and there was the monkey that had escaped from the zoo. It was walking along on its hind legs towards them. As it got closer, the zombies started trying to move faster. The monkey started running. The zombies literally dove through the bushes. Pete and Linda could hear all the noise the zombies were making as they continued trying to get away as fast as they could.

The monkey stopped, looked at Pete and Linda for several seconds, then he headed in the direction the zombies had gone. After he disappeared into the bushes Pete turned to Linda and said, "I would never have suspected zombies were terrified of monkeys. I'm sure glad they are, but I never heard about it before."

Linda's response, "You've got the engine running, let's get the blue blazes out of here. NOW!! And I never want to come back. I'm about to have a screaming fit. There are a lot of other restaurants we can go to in the future."

Pete quickly gunned the engine and exited the parking lot, in full agreement to never return to this place.

A week later Pete decided he was ready to go out and eat somewhere, but not at the zombie restaurant.

Linda was not quite as certain, but she finally decided they should go. They picked a restaurant on the other side of town they had been to some time ago.

Pete suggested, "This time let's park as near the front door as we can."

"Sounds good to me, Pete. I know it'll really help settle my mind."

With that, they hopped into the car and headed to the restaurant. At the restaurant, they stayed in the car while they looked all around the parking lot. There were no bushes capable of hiding something. All they saw was a storage shed.

"Things look really safe here. Let's go in and eat."

"Looks good to me too. Let's go."

Inside the restaurant they were seated after only a five minute wait. As they perused the menu they couldn't find some of the things they wanted, but they found enough things to entice them. They ordered and ate leisurely. After paying their bill they headed out to the parking lot, but first they opened the door slightly and looked out to see if they saw anything unusual. They didn't so they went out and walked toward their car. As they neared the car, the shed door burst opened. Linda screamed, "Pete. Get in the car. NOW!!"

Pete turned, looked, and yanked the car door lock switch out of his pocket, punched it to unlock all of the doors. They opened the two front doors, jumped in and Pete pressed the 'Lock All' button. As they sat there breathing heavily and watching, they saw three mechanical figures approaching.

"Those are robots, killer robots, Pete yelled. They can easily break the windows and get to us."

"Start the car. Get us out of here," Linda yelled.

Pete struggled to get the key in the ignition switch. He was trying to look at both the switch and the robots. Just then three cats came walking around the restaurant building. They paused, looked at the three robots, and started towards them.

The lead robot spotted the cats coming. He turned to the other two robots and waved a metal arm in the direction of the cats. All three robots stared at the cats as they came nearer, then they turned and headed back to the shed as fast as they could go, with the cats hurrying along behind them. The robots went into the shed and shut the door. The cats came up to the door and started sniffing around it.

Pete finally got the car started and accelerated out of the parking lot.

"Who knew killer robots were afraid of cats," said Pete.

"Maybe they're afraid the cat's claws can impact some of their electronic circuitry in a negative way."

"I can't think of any other reason for what just happened."

"Just be glad of it and keep driving."

Two weeks after the robot occurrence, Pete decided they would do a picnic in the city park. He felt this might be the safest way to eat out. He called Linda to tell her what he had decided and she tentatively agreed with him. She said, "I'll fix sandwiches and you can get the soft drinks and cookies. I'll see you at four-thirty this afternoon.

Pete checked his refrigerator to make sure he had enough bottles of soda. He did and he knew he had just bought a dozen chocolate chip cookies, so he had enough of those.

Meanwhile, Linda, at her home, started making sandwiches, two ham, two turkey, while thinking about seeing Pete again.

Both of them were whistling and singing as they got ready. They knew it was going to be a perfect sunny afternoon, and they would be together.

At four-thirty sharp Pete pulled into Linda's driveway. Linda came out, accompanied by her father who was carrying the cooler with the sandwiches. Her father greeted Pete, put the cooler in the back of the car, and said, "Good luck with this one, you two. Keep your eyes open, keep looking around, keep your keys handy, and have a great time."

Twenty minutes later, Pete and Linda pulled into the city park and found a picnic table. They set everything out on the table, sat down, and held hands for a while as they talked. Then Pete leaned over, kissed her, and said, "I brought the Frisbee. Let's toss it around for a bit. After ten minutes of Frisbee soccer, they decided to eat.

While they ate, they looking around, assuming anything could happen when they ate out.

As Pete was looking around, he noticed some movement on the walking path. He said, "Hey Linda, here come some walkers. They are moving right along. Maybe after we finish eating we could go for a walk."

Linda gave her approval of doing that, saying, "I know we both could use the exercise." She looked over at the walkers who had started moving along at a trot

"Pete, those aren't walkers. They look like vampires. I can't see their bared teeth to tell for sure."

Pete stood up and looked. "I think those are vampires. What are they doing in the city park?"

"Obviously they are looking for us. Right now we're the only sources of blood available."

"I'll collect up our stuff and we better get in the car."

"The devil with our stuff. Get in the car. NOW!!"

Pete grabbed Linda's hand and they ran for the car as the vampires quickly came at them.

"We're not going to make it to the car," Pete said.

About twenty yards away the tree limbs started shaking and a flock of bats came flying out of them. The bats started towards Pete and Linda.

Pete looked at the bats and said, "I've seen pictures of those things. They're vampire bats. There must be at least twenty of them. This whole place is after our blood. We may be goners."

The vampires turned to face the arriving vampire bats. With only two people present the two groups of vampires appeared to be ready to compete with each other for a chance at blood. The vampire bats turned and started flying toward the vampires. The vampires turned to flee from the bats. The bats caught up with the vampires and the two groups continued fighting as they went across the field, over the hill, and disappeared.

Pete and Linda grabbed what they could, got in the car, and drove out of the park. Neither of them wanted to talk about what had just happened. They did agree they wanted to eat at home for a while.

A month after the vampire event, Pete and Linda were sitting on the sofa at his place watching television. Pete said, "I may sound like a glutton for punishment, but I heard a very nice new restaurant has opened up in the mall. There's never any trees or bushes in a mall and you can usually see all around you. I think it might be a relatively safe place to eat. What do you think?"

"I guess I'm willing to give it a try, assuming we're very careful. Why don't we go tomorrow?"

"Okay with me."

The next day Pete picked Linda up and they headed for the mall. Neither one had much to say. They both kept looking around hoping they didn't see anything unusual as they pulled into the mall parking lot.

Linda said, "Boy, there sure are a lot of cars here in the lot. This place got popular quickly. I hope that's a good sign."

"It usually is. Plus, you don't see anybody running away from the place."

They headed into the restaurant. As they entered the front lobby, Pete looked towards the back of the restaurant. "Do you see all those people back there? They must be having some kind of get-together."

He looked over at the hostess's desk and saw a bulletin board sitting there. He stepped over to read it, then turned to Linda and said, "We better get out of here quick. If you think zombies, robots, and vampires are bad, this is probably the scariest of all."

"What is it? What's wrong? Tell me NOW!," Linda asked.

"The bulletin board says they have a group of politicians in here. It looks to be about twenty-five of them. Anybody who reads the newspaper or watches TV news knows politicians have a total lack of morals, they are completely self-serving, they only talk to the rich, and if you aren't rich you better not get in their way."

"I've seen it discussed on the news. Politicians will do anything for the one percent and they won't even talk to people like us."

Pete said, under his breath, "My God, let's get out of here."

"We're leaving right NOW!!", was Linda's answer.

Twenty years later they still didn't eat out more than once a month.

THANKSGIVING DINNER

"Hey, honey, how's Thanksgiving dinner coming along?"

"Doing very well, thank you, Dan. It will be ready soon."

"I hope you remembered I invited a few guests."

"How could I forget? You told me only three days ago. You've done this before, so I bought the biggest turkey the store had."

"Hmmm. Now I can really smell dinner cooking, Jane. It smells wonderful."

"I'll be taking things out of the oven very soon. It will all be on the table in about a half-hour."

Then came a knock at the front door.

"That must be some of the guests you invited. Why won't you tell me who they are?"

"I wanted them to be a surprise," Dan said as he walked to the door.

"Well, next time you can fix dinner for them and I'll dine over at Mother's.

When he opened the door Dan saw Frosty Snowman and Jack O'Lantern. Dan invited them in and asked if they wanted anything to drink. They both said no, commenting that it would freeze their mouths shut. Jane stood there with her open as she stared at them.

Frosty Snowman commented, "Boy, it's really warm in here. I'm dripping all over the place."

Jack O'lantern just stood there with a great big toothy grin on his face.

Another knock on the door rang out. Dan opened it and said, "Hey, Jack Frost is here. How did you know about our dinner?"

"Oh, Jack O'Lantern and I were just jacking around, and he mentioned it, so I invited myself."

As they all headed into the living room, Jack Frost turned to Jack O'Lantern and said, "Boy, is it ever warm in here. Can you ask Dan to turn down the heat? I'm leaving puddles of water everywhere. But the problem we have to settle first is who is going to be Jack-1 and who Jack-2 for the evening."

Jack O'Lantern said, "I would like to be Jack-1."

Frosty answered, "When we use the numbering system to differentiate between people with the same first name, the tallest person gets to be number one. Two is the next tallest and so on down the line."

Jack O'Lantern sat down at the table, obviously in a snit.

There came another knock at the door. Dan went over to open it and saw Scarecrow, who entered the room, shedding corn silks.

Dan quickly asked, "How did you know about our dinner?"

Scarecrow answered, "Jack O'Lantern was lying at my feet. He looked up at me and asked if I wanted to go to a special Thanksgiving dinner. Of course, I said 'Yes'."

Frosty Snowman quickly said, "Don't ask him anything that he can answer by shaking his head. You'll never get this place clean if you do."

Dan didn't even have time to step away from the door when another knock was heard. Dan opened it quietly, not wanting Scarecrow to try to hurry over and open it because of his shedding.

Dan thought, this must be a Troll and he's holding a box of donuts.

Frosty Snowman looked and said, "Don't you know donuts are for breakfast not dinner. I bet I know where you got them. I saw a Dunkin Donut sign just down the road."

Jane commented, "That can't be true. A Troll couldn't get into a Dunkin Donut store. They would stop him at the door because they grab as many as they can and start eating them."

The Troll suddenly tore open the box, grabbed a donut, and threw it at Frosty Snowman. Frosty grabbed a handful of mashed potatoes and threw it back at the Troll. Then everyone joined in for a food fight, with Jane screaming "Stop. Stop! I'll have to clean this mess up before we can eat."

No one paid attention until there was another knock at the door.

Then everybody pitched in to help clean the mess and they got it done in a very short time.

Meanwhile Dan went over and opened the door.

There on the doorstep was Dr. Phil. As he walked into the room, Scarecrow yelled, "Well, now that the Doctor is here, everything will be fine.

Dr. Phil responded, "That's what I do best. Fix everything up."

At the next knock on the door Dan said, "My God, who could this be?" When he opened the door, he was shocked to see six Elves.

One elf said, "Santa sent us over to get us out of his hair, particularly that long, white beard of his. He said he could get along without us for a few hours."

Dan asked, "How did he know about our dinner?"

Another elf replied, "Now, you know Santa knows everything."

A third elf asked, "When do we eat?", as he entered the room.

Jane said, "Very, very soon. Sit down at the table. We still have a lot of food left."

As they walking to the table there came another knock on the door. When Jane opened it, she stepped back thinking, "This must be Tom Turkey."

Tom stomped into the room saying, "Where is my twin brother? He was supposed to be here. Oh my God, is that him lying on the table? What have you done to him?" He then started pecking at anybody in reach, all the time yelling, "You killed him. You killed him."

After Tom had settled down and they were all seated at the dinner table, Jack O'Lantern and Jack Frost started talking about their interest in becoming authors. It turned out Jack Frost is writing his memoirs and Jack O'Lantern is writing a sexy novel about two pumpkins in love. He says he wants to finish it before he becomes a pumpkin pie.

Jack Frost said, "Hey, I heard about a group of people who want to be writers. They meet at Books and Company at the Mall. Maybe we could join them."

Scarecrow responded, "I think I'll write my memoirs. You would be surprised what I've seen in the cornfield."

Several hours later, after dinner, when all the guests were gone, Dan looked at Jane and said, "Now, that's what I call a Thanksgiving dinner."

Jane's reply was, "For Thanksgiving next year, let's eat out."

NO, NO

As John Merker sat on the cheap bed in his jail cell, he contemplated the end of his one year sentence. He had been caught trying to break into an ATM machine.

The ATM sat out, away from the bank itself. Even though it was two in the morning, there still was an occasional car driving by and the driver of one of these cars saw him swing something at the ATM, and the driver, apparently, traveled about a block down the road, pulled over, and called the police.

The police found John standing beside the ATM holding the sledge hammer with which he had only managed to make several big dents, but nothing sufficient to allow him to access the money inside.

The police had not used their sirens and so John had not been aware of their arrival until one of them walked up behind him, ordered him to drop the sledge hammer, and put his hands over his head.

John complied immediately, knowing he had no chance to run and trying to hit them with the hammer would be a very bad decision.

The police quickly handcuffed him, and put him in the back seat of the patrol car, and headed for jail. John was then put in a cell to await seeing a judge.

Four days later, John was taken before a judge to set a trial date. At his pre-trial appearance John decided it would be best if he pled guilty and asked for leniency. He thought he could handle everything himself.

John told the judge, "I wanted the money to pay off a gambling debt. I have vowed never to gamble again."

The prosecutor told the judge, "John Merker has accepted the terms of a plea agreement we offered him." The judge noted these things and said, "I would offer you the use of a pro-bono lawyer, but with the plea agreement I am prepared to proceed without one. John agreed to this and procedures started.

The judge noted this and the plea and said, "Since nothing was actually stolen, I will sentence you to only one year in prison with the proviso that you make restitution for the damage to the ATM. If you do not meet this proviso, you will be returned to prison for five years."

John replied, "I will meet the proviso."

"You're very fortunate. I am informed there was no internal damage to the ATM, so the cost will be the new cover, putting it on the machine, and completely checking to see if everything worked properly. This cost is estimated to be about four-hundred dollars. At this time you will be remanded back to jail to start your one year sentence. "Next case, please," and banged his gavel and John was led back to his jail cell.

As John found out, time moves slowly when your whole world consists of a small bed in an area about eight feet by eight feet. Even being taken out to the exercise yard once a day did nothing to help time move faster.

The only bright spot in his day was when the jail matron, Rebecca Wells, came once a month to meet with him about his crime and discuss his options when he was released.

John always pointed out he had learned his lesson and would never commit a crime again. He also pointed out his father a hardware store, and had told him there would be a paying job for him there when he was released. John told the matron this job promise would change his life, so he would never go to jail again.

As the year went on, John kept an eye on the young, very good looking matron and had started having dreams about her. As the end of his sentence approached, John engaged Rebecca in discussions about his life after jail. She seemed to be more and more interested in what he would be doing after he got out.

Finally, the day arrived. John was escorted to court by Rebecca and a policeman.

The judge listened carefully as Rebecca stated how John had been a very good prisoner over the year and that he had a job lined up after his release. "The prisoner is free to go," the judge said, banging his gavel.

Rebecca took John to a conference room to go over what would occur after his release. She stated, "Your limitations will be very few as long as you repay the four hundred dollars in a timely manner."

They discussed a monthly payment of fifty dollars which allowed him to pay it off in eight months.

As they finished up, John decided to take a chance and asked Rebecca if he could see her now that he was released.

She smiled at him and said, "John, you are an intelligent young man. You should certainly know you cannot end a sentence with a proposition."

REALLY?

S cott Malpin sat staring at his computer, knowing he had a great idea for a story that had been generated by a newspaper article about a lion attacking its keeper. However, he still had not come up with a usable title. He decided he should just start writing and see what came to mind, but he was still trying to come up with a title. He knew a really good title could help make a successful story. After a few moments thinking about a title he decided to start typing on his story.

'There existed a small area in Africa where the people of the Chasutu tribe had lived quite comfortably for generations. Hunting in their area was very good, water was plentiful from two small streams that flowed all year around, and many small trees and bushes were in the area to burn for fuel or for building homes.

One year as the women were collecting water for cooking, they noticed some things along the banks of the two rivers reflecting sunlight. This intrigued them and started them searching for the cause of the reflections. They found numerous pieces of a solid material causing the reflections, so out of interest they started collecting these. The people of the tribe used them primarily for decorations. Eventually, *as explorers and travelers passed through the area, it was discovered the reflectors were nuggets of gold. The word of the gold started to spread, and as a result people of all races and from all parts of the world came seeking their fortune from this resource that was proving to be widely available. These newcomers began to settle in the area, determined to seek their wealth. They slowly gained the trust of the tribesmen and eventually they were accepted by the tribe as friends and allies. As time passed these new people were also accepted as marriage prospects among the tribe, producing many multi-racial children. The town had become truly multi-racial in attitudes and appearances.'*

Scott realized he had a good start on his story, but he felt he had to take a break and let his mind work towards a title. The break also included supper as he heard his wife call out, "Everything's ready. Come on, let's eat."

After eating, Scott went back to his computer to work on his story. As he continued with it, his mind was still searching for the perfect title.

'One year there came a very hot, very dry summer. It was apparent the serious drought was affecting almost all of the animals in the area. What they needed to survive was getting in short supply. The small ones couldn't get enough plants and leaves to maintain themselves and the large ones couldn't get enough small animals to maintain themselves.

A large pride of lions was beginning to be seen coming and going in the outskirts of town. Obviously they were looking for a food supply and in this search, the lions entered the town on a regular basis, attacking everyone they came across, killing and eating the better parts of them. A few brave people tried to stop the lions, but the lions killed a lot of them, and those people then provided more food sources.

Finally, as the drought started to break, the lions moved on and the people who had survived this slaughter started to take stock of what had happened. It turned out fifty people had been killed and partially eaten.

The town knew it would survive this catastrophe, but it was quite a setback that would require a lengthy recovery time.'

As Scott sat back to think about his story his face suddenly lit up, he jumped up, waving his fist in the air, and yelled out, "I've got the perfect title, '*50 Shades of Prey*'. Now all I have to do is finish my story."

THE THREE FRIENDS

John and George sat in the Monter Bar and Restaurant recollecting some of the best and worst things that had ever happened to them. They were dressed as expected of college students; blue jeans, sweat shirts and tennis shoes. The people seated around them could hear them talking about the classes they were taking. They decided to share a story about the worst thing that had ever happened to them. They spent some time trying to decide whether to set some limits on the stories.

George said, "I have a lot of things I won't discuss with anyone. Let's limit it to Valentine's Day."

John responded, "I know a number of things you wouldn't want discussed. As you know I was involved in several of them. There was that time in Miami...."

"Shut up John or I'll bring up the time in Tampa when you and that police officer....."

"All right, all right. You win. We'll limit it to Valentine's Day. We need to wait for Phyllis to get here. She probably has a story of her own."

"Good idea."

Just then Phyllis came through the front door, glanced over and saw the guys sitting at the bar sipping their beers.

"Hey, there's an empty table over here. Let's sit down and be comfortable".

The two guys walked over and joined her. They had been friends for over ten years, and got together fairly often.

After they were all seated at the table, John and George explained the plans for the evening.

"Who is going to go first?" asked Phyllis.

"I will," John said. "I have a really good one to tell on myself. About twelve years ago, I was dating two girls. Neither knew about the other, and I wasn't going to tell them. I couldn't decide which one I liked better. Both were very pretty. I thought it was the perfect example of 'Hog Heaven'. Four days before Valentine's Day, I sent each of them a card. Inside each card was a note talking up our relationship in a very loving tone. I ran them down to the post office, put them in the mail drop, and gave a great sigh of relief at having got it all done. The day after Valentines, I got a call from Mary, one of the two girls. I assumed she wanted to tell me how much she liked the card and the note, but her first comment was 'You SOB'. She proceeded to thoroughly cuss me out and ended up asking me who in the devil Harriet was, and what was my relationship with her. She hung up without giving me a chance to say a word.

Ten minutes later I got a call from Harriet. She, also, opened up with a couple of curse words, demanded to know who Mary was. I stammered and searched for what to say, as she called me a fatherless human being. She slammed down the phone. I finally realized what had happened. I had put their cards in the wrong envelopes in my rush to get done."

"Well," said George, "they certainly had full understanding of what you were." Then he started to laugh as John tried to think of a good comeback.

"What happened after that? Were you ever able to explain it to either one of them?" Phyllis asked trying to suppress a laugh.

"No. They never talked to me again. They told everyone what a giant jerk I had been. I have been told the two of them are now the greatest of friends."

"How are you handling it now?" Phyllis asked. "Does it weigh heavily on your conscience?"

"Well it did for quite a while. A number of my friends started to make jokes about it. Things like asking how many girlfriends I have now. I've even had a few friends ask how many dates I've had lately and were all of them with the same girl. But I think it's time to move on to one of you two."

"I guess I'll go next although mine isn't as bad as yours, John," said George.

"Back in college I was dating this really nice, very good looking girl named Jessica. She was on the cheerleader squad and a straight A student. At the time we both were juniors. We had been dating for almost a year and it seemed to be developing into something serious. As I headed home for the weekend to see my parents I asked a friend to slip a Valentine's Day card under Jessica's dorm room door. Her roommate had gone home for the weekend as well so I didn't put Jessica's name on the envelope. In the card I had written several very romantic notes expressing my feelings for her. I also said Sunday evening when I got back from home we should meet at a specific restaurant near campus at five-thirty pm. Then I went home to see my parents whom I had not seen for three months.

Later, it all started to hit the fan. When I arrived back at campus, I quickly got cleaned up to meet Jessica at the restaurant. I got to the restaurant, was seated at a table, and ten minutes later, in walked Bell, the girl who has the room next to Jessica. She waved to me and came over. To my surprise she sat down.

She said, "That was a very nice Valentine's Day card you left for me. I didn't know you had those kinds of feelings for me. Particularly since you are dating Jessica."

As she talked, my jaw kept dropping lower and lower. She continued, "Also, it was convenient since I could not go home because of a project I had to have ready for Monday morning."

My jaw was about on the floor at this point. I just sat there stunned.

Bell said, "We had better order. I have to get back to my project." She continued, "You don't know it, but all the time you were dating Jessica, I felt you and I would make a great couple."

The more Bell talked, the more I discovered she was a very intelligent woman. Also very pretty. As she talked I started to realize just how nice she was. I also started to understand what had happened. My friend put the card under the wrong door, so Bell assumed it was for her.

We talked further as we ate. The more we talked, the more I was impressed with Bell. She was a junior and going for a B.S. in Physics. She also had hopes of attaining a PhD in Physics. I became more and more impressed with her. It almost made me ashamed I was only going for a B.S. in English and hoping to get a job teaching in one of the local high schools.

It was seven before when we left the restaurant and headed back to the campus. Bell had caught a cab to the restaurant, so I gave her a lift. We talked extensively on the way back, exploring each other's likes and dislikes. Hers turned out to be a good match to mine. It made me want to go for at least a Masters in English.

After I dropped her off at her dorm, I headed on to my dorm. I spent the entire evening, until after midnight, sitting in front of the TV with all kinds of thoughts running through my head. I was in a major state of confusion trying to figure out what to do. I finally decided to bite the bullet and do what my feelings and my brain were telling me needed to be done.

The next day I picked up Jessica and we went to lunch. We talked generally while we ate. I didn't want to say anything more while we were in the restaurant. After we ate, paid the bill, and went to the parking lot, I told her something strange had happened over the weekend.

"Jessica, I bought you a nice Valentine's Day card, and since I was going to be gone for a couple of days, I asked Steve to slide it under your door, but he put it under Bell's door next to yours."

"I was starting to wonder, because I never found a card and I sorta expected one."

"Well, since your roommate was out of town, I didn't bother to put your name on it. Bell assumed it was for her. In it I suggested we should meet at Doubledays, your favorite restaurant, when I got back. Bell, naturally, thought the card and the invitation were for her, so she showed up at Doubledays. We went ahead and ate dinner, talking all the while. I found out she is a very impressive and intelligent girl. We talked for over two hours, learning a lot about each other."

Jessica's face started to take on a dark look.

"What is all of this leading to? Tell me the truth."

"You and I have been dating for about a year, but I think we should start dating other people for a while. This is just to see if we are really meant for each other."

The dark look on Jessica's face got even darker, as she asked, "Does this mean you are breaking up with me?"

"I-I-I don't know what it means."

"I want to go back to the dorm, NOW!"

We did not talk to each other as we drove back. As soon as I pulled into the parking space, Jessica jumped out of the car and ran into the building. By the time I got out of the car, she was already in the elevator. I went back to my car, and headed back to my dorm."

As the three friends sat there waiting for George to finish, Phyllis asked, "What happened after that. I think I can guess.

George continued, "When I was back to my room I called Jessica. When she answered I got more cuss words than you did, John. Several years later, I heard that Jessica got married and now has two kids."

George and John looked at each other, looked at Phyllis, and looked back at each other.

Phyllis said, "Well I guess it's my turn."

John and George said in unison, "I hope yours is a nicer story than mine."

"Well, I'll tell it and let you decide."

"I think I'll need another beer," John said.

Immediately George responded, "Get me one also."

They both looked at Phyllis, but she said, "I'll get one after I tell my story."

When the two beers arrived, Phyllis started in. "By the time I was twenty-one I had dated several different boys, but I couldn't really get interested in any of them, for various reasons. The day before Valentine's Day my postman delivered a 'Special Delivery' package to door. We chatted for five or six minutes about different things of mutual interest. Then he took off to finish his delivery route.

The next day, Valentine's Day, I was out shopping for some clothes. As I entered a store, there stood the mailman holding packages of things he had bought. He looked quite different not dressed in his postal uniform. She almost didn't recognize him.

I said, "Hi."

He turned, saw me and said, "Hey there. I enjoyed our chat yesterday. I think I need a break. Would you like to join me for lunch?"

It turned out the package he had delivered to me was very important. It contained copies of pictures of my father my mother had made for me. My father had passed away two years earlier. Since I was already planning to go to lunch, I said yes.

As we talked and ate, we continued our discussion from the day before. His name was Phil, which I thought went well with Phyllis. He pointed out he had been delivering my mail for two years. My reply was 'I guess I wasn't paying much attention, but I was in college and not home a lot'.

We both could feel the natural attraction. He told me he had seen me a few times and had kept hoping to meet me and talk to me, but it hadn't happened. When we were leaving the restaurant, he asked me if I would like to go out with him. I said yes. He suggested getting together Saturday. I said O.K., and the process was started. Nine months later we were married. I am gloriously happy I found him."

"Well", George said, "if that's the worst that happened to you on a Valentine's Day, your best must be the time you hit the two hundred fifty million dollar lottery jackpot."

"You know that never happened. If it had I'd be sitting here dining with Robert Redford and Brad Pitt. No, I call it the worst because I could have talked to Phil two years earlier and would have had two more glorious years with him."

John said, "Next time let's talk about the best thing our parents ever did for us on a New Year's Day."

He looked at George and said, "That's when she'll tell us about that lottery ticket."

"Don't fool yourself. Even if I had won the lottery, I wouldn't tell you two."

"And here I thought we were friends."

With that Phyllis got up and headed for the door saying, "See you next time."

DREAMS

"Because there's nothing more beautiful
than the way the ocean refuses
to stop kissing the shoreline,
no matter how many times it's sent away."
– Sarah Kay

As I lie on the beach, listening to the unending waves as they roll up on the sand, the memories roll through my mind. Harriett, our life together had been ideal in every way. Thinking back on our sixty years together, I realize how lucky I was to find you and to convince you to marry me, but sixty years wasn't nearly long enough to be with you.

Our marriage ceremony was most beautiful, as all those who were there have told us many times over the years. Our love was deep except for a few minor disputes. I remember our biggest quarrel. We were deciding where to move to in our new city. I wanted an apartment and you wanted a house. I really did like the house we bought.

We first met in the eighth grade. I played on the boy's baseball team and you played on the girls' soccer team. I was the third best batter on my team, but you were the star scorer of your soccer team. I thought you might not want to talk to me since I was only third best. Because of this, our friendship didn't start in earnest until the ninth grade. Three years later I was finally able to win you over and we were married right out of high school.

I went to work in my father's garden supply store, but your job choices were greatly diminished since you were pregnant before our first anniversary came around. Shortly into our second year our first child, Harry, was born. He was followed over the next five years by Mary and Rebecca, both of whom strongly resembled you, and become beautiful young ladies.

Over the many years we had an enjoyable, relaxed life, not rich, not poor. My income was always in the comfortable range, and then more than comfortable after I took over my father's business. The brightest joy in our lives, as we grew older, were our five grandkids, Harry Jr., Brian, Harriett, Martin, and Rebecca, who was named after her mother. By our 60th year we had two great-grand kids, Harry III and William.

Lying here on the beach, thinking of the past and the future, my thoughts are like the waves. They persist, just as my love for you persists.

We were married for sixty years and I wanted it to go on forever. I am still deeply in love with you. Like my love for the sea, my love for you is eternal.

When you left me, I knew it wasn't your choice. Cancer took you away from me. Now that I have had my second heart attack, I am looking forward to joining you and asking you to marry me again.

With that he closed his eyes and went to be with her forever, and the waves continued kissing the beach.

THE ANNIVERSARY GIFT

David said, "Honey, I know it's a tragedy, but we had no choice. He was in great pain and the best thing we could do for him was to take him to the vet and painlessly euthanize him. He was one of the best cats we ever had, but he was in so much pain."

Helen replied, "I understand all of that David. It had to be done, but I loved him so much. I agree he was the best cat we ever had. The all-white fur and the blue eyes are very rare in cats. We will never find another like him. I will miss him for a very long time, maybe forever."

"Please don't say those things, honey. Many, many homeless cats out there would love the kind of good home we have always provided. I fully understand your feelings about losing Bear, but I'm not prepared to say we will never have another cat. I can name several places we could walk into and almost immediately find a cat we could love almost as much as Bear."

"I understand, but I'm not ready to hear it, let alone think about it. Please don't bring it up again."

"I promise I won't mention it again, Helen. I need to get back to work now. Try to relax. I'll be home about five-thirty and we can go to dinner somewhere nice. How about the Steak Shack? They have really good food there."

"That would be nice. We haven't been there since you took me there on our eighth anniversary. I really enjoyed it. Maybe it will help settle my mind on all of this."

David left for work and all the way there he was trying to think what would be the best thing for him to do. He knew he would miss Bear about as much as his wife did, but he had to concentrate on easing the whole situation. As he was driving into the parking lot at work, an idea popped into his head. It was six months until their tenth anniversary and he was getting a bonus at work in five months. He wanted to tie all of this together in a really nice way. He felt he needed to give it a lot of thought.

As time went by, David kept thinking of things he could do and rejecting them for one reason or another. Finally he realized what he had to do, and their tenth anniversary was the perfect time to do it.

Five months later, when he had received his bonus check, he put his plan into action. On his way home from work he deposited the certified check in his savings account, knowing the money would be available within two days.

Three days later David stopped at a jewelry store on his way home. It only took him fifteen minutes to pick out a nice ring with a one-quarter carat diamond set in it. When he got home he hid the ring in his underwear drawer, knowing Helen never looked in there. She laundered his underwear but always let him fold it up and put it away. He knew it would be safe in there for a month.

He then took Helen to the Bob Evans Restaurant for supper. She was now a little more relaxed about losing Bear, but mention of him still brought tears to her eyes.

Four weeks later on her anniversary, David stopped at the Petsmart store. He had checked them the previous day and found they had a six month old white kitten with green eyes for adoption. David bought the kitten, a carrier, a litter pan, and a bag of litter, then he made arrangements to pick all of it up the next day.

When he went into the store to pick up the kitten, he noticed a grey-tiger kitten with blue eyes. He thought to himself, *I shouldn't do this, but the blue eyes complete things.* He bought a second carrier, put the two kittens in their carriers, and got everything out into the back seat of the car.

When David got home, he parked in the driveway, rolled down the windows so the kittens could get air, and went into the house.

Helen was sitting on the sofa, all ready to go to the Steak Shack. David said, "Hi", kissed her and said, "I've got a couple of things to do before we go to eat". He went into the bedroom and got the diamond ring and put it in his jacket pocket. Next he went out to the car and brought the two kittens into the living room. He set them down on the floor.

Helen drew in a deep breath, threw her hands up into the air and gave David a very angry look. Just as she started to say something, the white kitten climbed up on the sofa, petted his head against her leg, climbed into her lap, curled up and lay down. The cat started to purr. At that moment the grey tiger jumped onto the sofa and tucked in against Helen's leg.

Helen's angry look disappeared as a tear drop appeared in her left eye. As the tear rolled down her cheek, she picked up the white kitten, held him up, and looked into his face. More tears rolled down her cheeks as she moved the kitten against her cheek and hugged him tightly. Again the kitten purred and licked her cheek once, twice, three times.

Helen reached down and picked up the grey tiger, raised him to her other cheek and hugged him. She turned to David and said, "We'll call them Whitey and Tiger."

David moved over to her saying, "I have one more thing for you to show my love. He reached down and carefully slid the diamond ring on her finger. He said, "I know the tenth anniversary is not the diamond one but I thought you deserved one. We'll do the Steak Shack tomorrow after we get the kittens settled."

With tears rolling down her cheeks and two kittens purring, Helen looked at David and said, "Thank you honey. I love you so very much."

THE RESCUE

"**D**onna! Look across the street."

"Bill, is this important? I'm hungry."

"Look at what I see and then tell me if you think it's important."

Donna turned slowly as she chewed a bite of her hamburger. She saw a little boy, about five or six years old, standing on the sidewalk looking around.

She asked, "How long has he been standing there?"

"About ten minutes, I think. No adults have been around there. I think he may be either lost or abandoned."

The little boy turned and headed back down the alley.

"He must be going home, finally," said Bill.

As the couple ate, they kept looking across the street to see if the little boy showed up again. He didn't, so they were relieved assuming he had gone home.

Two days later, at the same restaurant, the little boy showed up again, and again just stood there looking around.

Bill asked the waitress, "Have you seen this little boy across the street before? How often does he come there and just look around?"

The waitress replied, "I've seen him there a few times, but I usually work the morning shift and I don't remember seeing him in the morning. Do you know anything about him?"

Donna asked, "Bill, do you think we should go check on him?"

"Maybe we should just call the police."

The waitress commented, "I know of one time, he was out there and a police car went slowly past. The boy quickly disappeared back into the alley and didn't come out for some time. From that I assume he doesn't want to have anything to do with the police."

"You're probably right. We have to find out what's going on. We need to think of the best way to approach him so we don't scare him away."

"Why don't you just call Child Protective Services (CPS) and let them handle it?" the waitress asked.

"I may have a reasonable way of doing an initial check on him," said Donna. "We can't just go out the front door and across the street. He'll disappear in a hurry. I suggest we go out the back door and circle around the block so he thinks we are just people out shopping. We need to appear to be ignoring him completely as we approach."

Bill and the waitress agreed this would be the best thing to try. Bill and Donna settled their tab and the waitress led them through the kitchen to the back door. They circled around two blocks and headed down the street to where the boy was still standing. As they approached him, they tried to maintain a very casual attitude, talking to each other, pointing things out, and pausing to look at things.

The boy moved back to the entry way of the alley, but didn't run away.

As they got closer, the boy stayed, obviously watching them. Bill and Donna stopped and looked across the street. Bill pointed at the restaurant, then Donna turned to the boy and asked, "Do you know if that's the utility store over there?"

He stared at them for a few seconds, and finally said, "No, it isn't. I know that's a place to get food."

"Do you know if the food is good?"

"I really don't know."

Donna looked at Bill and said, "I could use a piece of pie. How about you?"

"Sounds good to me."

Then he turned to the boy and asked, "Would you like to join us for a piece of pie or a sandwich?"

"Yes. I would. A sandwich sounds good, but I don't have any money."

"I'm buying. Why don't you join us?"

"Ok. I'd like to."

All three started across the street heading for the restaurant. As they went in the maître-de looked at them and started to say something.

Bill quickly raised a finger to his lips in the well-known symbol 'Shush'. The maître-de paused and then said, "Welcome. Would you like a booth or a table?"

Donna said, "A table would be great, thanks."

The maître-de picked up three menus, led them to a table, and said, "Your waitress, Amy, will be here shortly."

Bill tried to make a joke and said, "You mean we can't have a tall waitress?"

Only Bill and the boy giggled at the attempt. Donna and the maître-de looked at each other and just shook their heads. The maître-de left to tend to the front door, shaking his head all the way there. Bill and Donna couldn't see it but when he reached the podium area, he had a great big smile on his face and was struggling to not laugh out loud.

A few minutes later Amy came walking up and asked, "Are you ready to order?" She didn't say anything else, but she looked at Bill and Donna who had just eaten there and you could tell she was thinking, *They got the boy to come eat. Maybe they can find out who he is and what's going on.*

Donna asked the little boy, "What would you like?"

He replied, "Yes. I want a hamburger, French fries, and a piece of peach pie with ice cream. Oh yes, and a coke to drink."

The waitress looked at Bill and Donna and asked, "What will you folks have?"

Bill replied, "Well, I was thinking of a T-bone steak and a big baked potato with everything on it. But I will settle for a piece of that peach pie, but I like mine without ice cream."

The waitress said to Bill, "Ice cream really enhances the flavor of the peach pie."

Bill said, OK, you have convinced me. I'll have ice cream with my pie."

Donna said, "I'll have what he's having. Peach pie and ice cream. Can you hold off on our pie until this young man is ready for his?"

"Certainly." She turned and headed for the kitchen to put in the orders. Bill got up saying, "On second thought I want some coffee too." He then headed after the waitress. As she approached the door to the kitchen Bill caught up with her and asked her if she could call CPS and tell them what was going on.

As they waited for the boy's burger and fries to come they engaged him in conversation as best they could. Their first comment was to tell him they were Bill and Donna Albertson and then ask, "What's your name and how old are you?"

I'm Tommy Kelson, and I'll be six years old soon."

"When's your birthday?"

"In August. What's today's date?"

"This is mid-July, so you have a few weeks to your birthday, Tommy."

"When's my food coming? I'm hungry. I want my burger, fries, and pie."

"Well, they should be here soon. By the way, where are your parents? Do you have any relatives around here, like brothers, sisters, or grandparents?" Bill asked.

"I don't know of any. My mom has gone somewhere. I don't know where. Daddy's gone. I can tell you where he's buried, if you want to go there."

"I don't think we need to do that just now, Tommy."

"I remember my mom saying her sister was somewhere out west. I think it was California."

Anxiously Bill asked, "Do you remember a name being said or a place in California?"

"No. I don't remember."

Tommy said he had to go to the bathroom, and while he was gone Bill and Donna could talk freely about what to do.

Bill said, "His aunt lives about a thousand miles from here and we would never be able to locate her. We have to think what else we can do. Obviously we need to get CPS involved as quickly as possible."

Donna said quietly, "I think we need to contact Children's Services. It may be the best thing we can do for him."

"I'm not sure that would be best for him," Bill said. "He's already gone through a lot of tragedy. We need to learn more about what has been going on with him, how he's been surviving."

"Let him finish eating, then we will ask him some more questions."

Tommy got back to the table just as his meal arrived. He sat down and started eating and while he ate Donna asked, "Tommy, can you tell us where you've been eating and sleeping?"

"Sure. These restaurants around here always have some good food in the trash cans. I guess people don't eat all their meal and it gets thrown out."

"That's probably not good for you. Where do you sleep?"

There's a place near here that's open all night. Their backdoor is always warm. I sleep close to it."

"I think I know where it is. We need to find some place for you to stay at night. Our place only has one bedroom, but we do have a sofa you could sleep on. I have to tell you that we need to talk to somebody about you. Is that OK?"

"I don't know. Am I going to jail?"

"Absolutely not", said Donna. "They will just help us find your family or a place to stay."

"We need to make sure you are safe and fed properly and regularly," responded Bill.

The waitress came back and indicated for Bill to come talk to her. They went over to the other side of the room. As they stood by the far wall, the waitress said she had called the CPS number and got a recording telling her to call the police if it was an emergency.

Bill went back to the table and said he knew there was a police station five blocks away, and he suggested they head there to talk to somebody. Donna took Tommy's hand and they headed for the station. When they got there they started to tell Tom's story to the officer behind the desk, but he very quickly led them into Captain Johnson's office. They talked to the captain, telling him everything they knew about Tommy and his situation.

Captain Johnson thanked them for jumping in and helping Tommy. He then, called CPS and left a message for them to call him. He next asked if Bill or Donna had any suggestions about where to go from here.

Bill answered, "We might propose, that Tommy stay with us for now. He can sleep comfortably on our sofa, and we will see that he is well fed and safe until things can be ironed out. A true foster home would probably be a much better arrangement for him in the long run, and I would guess that is what CPS will recommend."

Captain Johnson stepped out to the front desk and asked the officer there to run a computer check on Bill and Donna Albertson. He, also, asked him to take Tommy on a tour of the police station, he needed to talk to Bill and Donna about something without Tommy present. The officer did a quick computer check and found nothing bad. He went back in, gave the computer printout to Capt. Johnson and then asked Tommy if he would like a tour of the place. Tommy seemed excited to do that, so the two of them headed out. Capt. Johnson told Bill and Donna, "A woman was found comatose on the street. She was taken to hospice and she died two days later. She had no identification on her and they have never figured out who she was. Maybe this could be the boy's Mother. I understand and agree with what you are saying, but we have procedures we have to follow. We have an officer in this station who regularly deals with the family office. He's out on a call right now, but I'll check with him as soon as I can and I'll relay the information to you as soon as I have it. For now, why don't you two go ahead and take the young man with you so we know he's safe."

"OK. We'll do that and we'll wait until you have the information. Here is our address and phone number. Since tomorrow is Saturday, we should be home most of the day", Bill said as he pulled his car keys out of his pocket.

On the drive home Bill and Donna explained to Tommy what was happening. He indicated he did understand and said he would be happy with whatever they worked out as long as he didn't have to sleep in the alley anymore.

When they got home, they turned on the TV for Tommy and Donna started fixing supper.

At eight o'clock, all of them were watching the Comedy Channel when the phone rang. Bill answered it, and said "Hello, Captain Johnson. Did you talk to the Foster Plan guy?"

Captain Johnson said, "I've talked to him and we've set up an appointment for you on Monday at three PM."

Bill replied, "We will be there."

After hanging up, Bill told Donna and Tommy what was going on. They understood this weekend would be for them to enjoy, before Tommy moved to a more permanent arrangement. Both Bill and Donna assured Tommy that wherever he went they would visit often. At this his eyes beamed with happiness.

They spent the weekend at the zoo, in the park, riding the miniature train, going horseback riding, and many other activities. By Sunday evening all three of them were happy to have supper at home and go to bed early.

Monday morning they had a late breakfast, and prepared to go to the police station. At the station Captain Johnson greeted them and then took them into Lt. Harrison's office and introduced them. He also introduced the CPS representative, a Mrs. Joanne Burke. With that they started discussing the information the lieutenant had found.

Lt. Harrison started by telling them to call him Jim. Then he got into what he had to offer.

"I spent several hours Saturday going through my listing of foster families, and I have three that look like good candidates. Mrs. Burke agrees with my findings. The first family has a boy less than a year older than Tommy, which would probably work out well. The second family has two children, a boy two years older than Tommy and a girl four years older. This would probably be our third place choice of the three families, because Tommy would be the youngest of the three, and this may not be the best thing..

The third family is a young couple, married ten years with no children as of yet. They wish to have children, but haven't yet been successful. Of the first and third families, I would rate them about even. I think either one would make a great foster family for Tommy. It will come down to a few details. The primary one being the father in the first family travels a lot and I think Tommy needs a father figure around at his age. For this reason I am recommending the third family. The wife is a stay at home and the husband has a local job that doesn't require travel. I've discussed this with Mrs. Burke, and she agrees completely, this third family would make an excellent choice. Would all of you like to go and meet this family?"

Bill and Donna nodded yes, and Tommy just looked around at everybody, uncertain of what to do.

Lt. Harrison called the chosen family, David and Rhonda Billson, and set up an appointment for all of them to be at his office Wednesday at 6:00 pm.

On Wednesday everyone showed up on time and were ushered into Lt. Harrison's office. Introductions were made all around. During all of this the Billsons were starting to get to know Tommy and vice-versa. The Billsons seemed to get along quite well with Tommy and Tommy finally seemed to get relaxed and start to talk easily with them.

After thirty minutes Lt. Harrison asked the Billsons if they were willing to foster Tommy. They replied they had a good impression of Tommy and were willing to do so. Lt. Harrison then asked Tommy what he thought of being fostered by them. He said he liked them and it would probably be OK.

Tommy then expressed his main concern, "Will I ever see Bill and Donna anymore?"

Bill and Donna said together, "Yes, you will see us." Donna continued, "We will come visit you as often as we can. We would miss you greatly if we didn't."

As the meeting was coming to an end, Lt. Harrison said to the Billsons, "Since the Albertsons both work and it will take us about four days to finalize the paperwork, can you take Tommy in for those four days?"

David and Rhonda said together, "Absolutely." David asked if they could go by the Albertsons and pick up Tommy's stuff. "We have a nice bedroom for him to settle into."

"Why don't you follow us to our place and we can gather up what Tommy has," said Bill. "Then we can follow you to your places. We will then know where you live and we can help you get Tommy settled in."

"Sounds good to me. Shall we go", Rhonda asked.

They went to their cars and drove to the Albertson's house. It took less than half an hour to pack up Tommy's clothes. They, then, headed to the Billson's house and got Tommy's things moved into the bedroom he would be using. Tommy supervised putting his clothes in a dresser, making sure he knew where everything was.

Everyone sat down in the living room and talked for an hour. Then they asked Tommy to go into his room and put on his pajamas. After he had done this, they all went in to tuck him into bed.

Bill and Donna said, "Goodbye", and told him they would be back tomorrow night to see him. David and Rhonda said goodnight, they would see him in the morning.

Back in the living room, the Albertsons and the Billsons talked about Tommy, his needs, what school he would attend, and if there were other children nearby for him to play with.

Satisfied with all the answers, Bill and Donna were ready to go home and get some rest. Just before they left, they stepped into Tommy's room and said, "Goodbye, till tomorrow."

Tommy grinned and said, "OK." He knew he would not be losing his new friends.

TO MOCK A KILLING BIRD

T wo squirrels, named Randy and Dickie, sat on a limb of a maple tree, twenty feet up in the air. It was a nice warm sunny day and they had enjoyed lunch under the oak tree about fifteen feet away. They were now resting, digesting their food, and enjoying the good life of squirrels.

Randy looked up into the sky, turned to Dickie and indicated for him to look up. Both of them watched as a hawk circled around for a few minutes. They knew the hawk was looking for a small animal to eat.

The two squirrels looked at each other and smiled. Randy thought, *'Let's have some fun. That hawk would eat whichever of us he could catch, but I think we can have some fun, and get away alive,'* and Dickie understood him completely. Dickie carefully made his way to a nearby hollow tree with a hole in it, while Randy stayed in the first tree which also had a hole in the trunk.

Randy started jumping around to tempt the hawk. When the hawk dove, he ducked into the hole in his tree and Dickie popped out of the other tree, and started to make a lot of noise. The hawk changed direction to that one. Randy popped out again as Dickie dashed back into hiding. The hawk changed direction again. They got the hawk to change direction six times, then both squirrels went into their respective holes and stayed there. The hawk perched on a limb looking back and forth, then finally took off and soared skyward.

They went through this routine two more times with at least five changes per each dive. The hawk, now tiring of all of this, flew away to find something else to eat.

The next day the whole game was repeated with the same result as the first day. The hawk, again, flew elsewhere to look for food.

The squirrels sat on a limb together, high fiving in a squirrely manner. They assumed they had won a total victory.

A week later the hawk was back and he apparently had figured things out. He first dove at Randy, then immediately changed course to where Dickie would pop out. Dickie saw him coming and changed course so fast he nearly fell off the limb, but he managed to hold on and make it back into his hole. Both of the squirrels decided it might be time to quit the game as the hawk seemed to be smarter than they thought.

Three days later the hawk was back and the squirrels decided if they were more cautious they could continue the game. But it turned out the hawk had gained further knowledge of what was going on. On his third dive, he headed for the tree where Randy was expected to pop out. As he approached the tree Randy started to come out, saw the hawk coming at him and ducked back in, just in time.

Randy stuck his head out and started making as loud a noise as he possibly could. In squirrel talk he was cussing out the hawk. The hawk promptly headed somewhere else to try to obtain lunch more easily.

The two squirrels had peace and quiet for now. They had great hopes the hawk had permanently found better hunting somewhere else.

Two weeks later, the squirrels were sitting on a tree limb, discussing in squirrel talk, the great weather they were having and what they were going to have for lunch. Both were quite pleased that apparently their chances of being lunch had been greatly reduced. Suddenly they saw a blue jay fly into the tree, land on a limb, and snuggle up close to the trunk. The squirrels started looking around to see what was happening. When they looked up they saw the hawk in a dive and he was really close. The two squirrels, at the same time, dove for the hole in the tree. Randy, the first one there, moved out of the way as best he could. The hawk grabbed the end of Dickie's tail with his beak. Dickie had almost made it completely into the safe hole. From there it became a tug of war, the hawk grasped the limb as tight as he could with his talons, and pulled on Dickie's tail, while Dickie grasped the inside of the tree with his claws.

The tug of war lasted for a couple of minutes with neither gaining an advantage. Finally the hair of Dickie's tail pulled loose. The hawk fell back but he maintained his grip on the limb. Dickie dropped as deep into the hole as was possible, making sure he pulled his tail in behind him.

The hawk moved over to the entrance of the hole and peered into it, but he couldn't get far enough in to get hold of either squirrel. Finally he flew off, and was last seen leaving the area.

Randy and Dickie stayed in the hole until dusk and finally stuck their heads out to look around. They saw the hawk was gone, so they came out, but stayed close to the hole.

The hawk never came back and the two squirrels lived happily for the rest of their natural lives.

DOG GONE

Dogs Do Think

"It's your turn, Mable!"

"No. It's your turn, Charles. I've done it the last two times."

"I think you're making that up, but I'll go ahead and feed the dogs anyway. They're out in the backyard right now. I'll take the food out there to them."

Charles went into the kitchen to get the food bowls ready and then he stepped out the back door calling, "Butch, Shorty, come on". As he set the bowls down, the two dogs raced to him. The German Shepherd, named Butch, easily beat the Lhasa Apso, named Shorty, to the bowls, but when the Lhasa got there he quickly shoved the much bigger Shepherd away from the bowl he had started to eat from, and Butch had to go to the other bowl. Shorty obviously ruled the place and the Shepherd let him.

As he moved to the other bowl, the Shepherd was thinking, *I don't know why I allow him to do that. I could eat him in two bites. But he is a nice dog. I like him, I guess.*

After they had eaten, the two dogs started to romp around the yard. They had a number of toys they liked to play with when they were outdoors. Butch had to be careful. As he would start to grab a rubber ball, Shorty would charge in and try to grab the same one. Butch almost grabbed Shorty several times by mistake. He knew that could hurt Shorty so he held back, even though he was tempted several times to go ahead and grab him.

As they played with their toys, racing back and forth across the yard, Butch bounced off the fence next to the gate and the gate swung open. Butch stepped into the gate area, looked around and saw two birds. Without hesitation he took after them. When he saw two more birds a little farther away, he decided to go after them. As he was charging towards those two birds he saw a larger group of birds down the street and went after them. Very quickly he was more than ten blocks from home. He started to look around, and thought, w*here am I? What happened? How do I get back home?* Butch did the only thing he could think of doing at that point. He started running through the neighborhood, searching for a way back home.

With a big German Shepherd running through the neighborhood it didn't take long for someone to call the Humane Society and ask them to come get him. They asked if he had bitten anyone. The answer was 'No, he's just running around like he's lost'. The Humane Society person said they would be there as soon as they could, and asked the caller to try to keep track of the dog so they could find him easily.

The Humane Society van showed up quickly and they went immediately to the address of the man who had called them and asked if he could point them to where the dog might be now.

The man said, "I saw him about two blocks east of here fifteen to twenty minutes ago. He'd apparently found something to eat and appeared to be throwing himself into eating it."

"What kind of dog is it?"

"It's obviously a German Shepherd and he doesn't seem dangerous at all."

"That's all good information. It will really help us in capturing him, but we always make sure we play it safely. Thanks for your information. We'll go look for him."

With that the two Humane Society guys headed to where the Shepherd was last seen. From a block away they could see Butch lying on the sidewalk still chewing on what he had found. The two approached him carefully, not wanting to disturb him too much. Butch looked up when the two guys came within ten feet of him, but then he went back to eating. The two got within five feet and quickly slipped a noose on an eight foot pole over his head and tightened it enough that Butch could not get free. Butch jumped up but then just looked at the two while shaking his head trying to throw off the noose.

With the noose in place, the two of them started working Butch over to the van. It didn't take long to get him in the back of the van, loosen the noose, slip it over Butch's head, shut the door, and hop into the front seats. They then headed for the Humane Society Shelter. Once there, they easily got Butch into one of the cages, where he and they would be safe.

Meanwhile, back at home, Charles said, "I think I should go check on the dogs. They should have finished eating and will have played themselves out."

Charles went out the back door, calling the dogs to come. He saw Shorty sitting by the fence, but couldn't find Butch. Then he saw the open gate and pushed his panic button. He ran over, closed the gate, grabbed Shorty, and hurried back into the house, calling for Mable to come help.

Upon hearing about the open gate and the missing dog, Mable also pushed her panic button.

"Quick, get in the car," Mable said. "We have to go looking for Butch."

They got in their car and spent two hours driving around the neighborhood, with no sign of Butch. Back home, they spent a very unhappy evening, finally going to bed at eleven that evening. As they lay in bed, Mable started softly crying. Charles moved over and hugged her tightly saying, "We'll find him tomorrow. It's Saturday and we can spend the entire day looking for Butch. I know it's tough, but try to get some sleep tonight."

Mable spent another hour worrying, but finally dropped off to sleep.

The next morning Charles and Mable had breakfast and went out immediately to search for their missing dog. After four hours covering the whole neighborhood with no luck at all, they went back home to determine what their next step should be. As they sat in their living room discussing possibilities, Mable suddenly stood up and said, "Charles, we need to see if anyone has taken Butch to one of the animal rescue places. The Humane Society place is over on Main Street. We could start there. I know of two other places we can check with also. Let's go."

Once again they hurried to their car and headed for the Humane Society building. As they drove along Mable kept saying softly, "Please, please, let Butch be there safe and sound."

Meanwhile, as they approached Main Street, Butch was walking around his cage thinking, *I've got to get out of here somehow and go home. I'm not comfortable here. I don't know if there is any way I can just sneak out. I've got food and water, but this is not a good place to be. I don't know what all can happen to me here. I've heard very little about it. That pug from down the street from my home was in here once and he was telling me some strange things about it.*

Charles and Mable pulled into the Humane Society parking lot and headed into the building. As they went in, Butch's head suddenly jerked up in the air and he started sniffing as hard as he could. He thought, *I smell Mommy and Daddy. They've come to take me home. I know they are. I knew they would.*

As they walked up to the front counter, Mable asked, "Have you picked up a German Shepherd? I really hope you have. Please say yes."

The man behind the counter looked at them for a couple of seconds and said, "Yes. We picked one up yesterday. Would you like to see if he is the one you're looking for?"

Together Charles and Mable said, "Yes, please."

As they walked into the back room Butch was about to knock his cage over, he was jumping so hard.

Charles ran over to the cage, saying, "Thank goodness. It is our Butch. Please let him out of the cage so we can take him home."

When the cage door was opened Butch ran out and jumped up on Charles, licking his face as fast as he could.

Charles paid the fee to free Butch, then thanked the Humane Society guy, and took their dog out to the car. As they drove home, Butch kept trying to climb into the front seat to sit on Mable's lap. Finally, at home, they took Butch in and the two dogs started romping together and running from room to room.

Finally Charles said, "This calls for a reunion party." He got out some pieces of steak for the dogs and poured glasses of wine for himself and Mable.

As the dogs ate the steak, Shorty thought, h*ey, this is worth you getting lost. Can you do it again?*

Butch reached over and nipped Shorty's ear thinking, d*on't ever say that again.*

Shorty quickly apologized thinking, I'll *never bring it up again.*

MIGHTY YAR

"Come on you guys, let's try to get this racing started while we have good wind. Oh, I'm sorry, we have two guys still trying to get their boats ready. I guess we'll hold for ten more minutes, then we'll start without them. They can take a 'Did Not Start' for the first couple of races."

Fifteen minutes later all of the boats were in the water and ready to go.

Bob looked over at Jim and said, "I love this radio control (R/C) sailboat racing. It's the most fun I've ever found. Of course, that's assuming your boat is running well and you're not finishing last in every race. I've had that happen before, but today I'm planning on beating John to the finish line a few times."

"All I can say is good luck. He's the best racer in the club and almost always winds up in first or second place overall after the racing is done," replied Jim.

The race director (R/D) called out, "Is everybody ready to go? I'm going to start the countdown to begin the race."

He pushed the button to start the countdown, and every boater started trying to get into a position allowing him to hit the start line with the most advantage on starboard tack.

Everything went this way for the first five races, then the race director called for a fifteen minute break for retuning or whatever the racers might need to do. Usually at least four of them pulled their boats out and made a dash for the bathroom. Most of them just pulled their boats out and relaxed for fifteen minutes.

As the break ended and the racers were scrambling to get their boats back into the water, a car pulled into the parking lot and a young lady emerged. Immediately most of the racer's eyes were distracted away from their boats causing some bumping into each other. This was true for the boats as well as the boaters. It was rare to have someone come out to watch, let alone someone who attracted so much attention.

The race director called out, "Watch your boats, idiots, not the spectators, and get ready for the next race. The countdown will start in two minutes. Make sure you're ready."

As the boats circled for the start, the young lady made herself comfortable on one of the benches and prepared to watch.

At the start bell Bob held the best position at the line. He was at the starboard end of the line and a few inches ahead of John and Jim. Bob started yelling, "I'm starboard, I'm starboard. Stay clear. I'm starboard."

All obeyed the rule and all left the start ready to fight for the best position approaching the first mark, which was fifty feet away. Bob maintained his starboard position as they approached the first mark and managed to gain fifteen more inches lead on John, as Jim dropped back to fourth place.

Jim tried to keep from cursing as another boat failed to yield to his starboard position. Instead he just yelled' "Foul. Foul. Boat number 675 fouled me". A call that was immediately echoed by the race director.

Boat 675, which was being sailed by John, immediately started its three-hundred-sixty degree penalty turn. John acted like he wanted to argue about whether he had committed a foul, but in reality he knew he had, and he knew this penalty turn would cost him this race.

Bob, while trying to suppress a large grin, knew this could give him this race, and a tie for first in the race standings.

As they finished the race, the results were Bob-first, Jim-third, and John seventh.

John came back in the next race, trying to make up for his error in the previous race. He led the fleet by six lengths as he crossed the finish line, and he didn't try to suppress his grin. He knew he now had the overall lead by two points over Bob.

After four more races, the RD called for a fifteen minute time-out for retuning the boats because of wind speed changes.

During the break, the young lady came over to Bob and asked, "How many more races will you do today?"

Bob stammered for a second before answering, "We usually try for twenty races each time out. Usually we get them in. It depends on weather and the wind of course."

As they stood there talking, Bob could feel his knees getting weaker. He thought, *I think this is the most beautiful girl I've ever met.*

He finally gathered himself together enough to say, "I'm Bob Hurley. I've been racing these boats for over ten years now. It's one of the most enjoyable things in which I ever got involved with." Then, as his chest swelled noticeably, he said, "Next year, I'm going to be president of this club."

"Congratulations. My name is Mary, Mary Carson. I'm quite fascinated by these R/C boats. I saw them being raced when I was in Florida five years ago and I've been wondering if there was a local club. Then I saw the mention in the newspaper of your club racing today, and I thought I would come out and watch."

"We usually have a few practice/play heats after the official racing is done. Would you like to try sailing one of the boats?"

Her instant response was, "I would love to. I have flown an R/C airplane for a few minutes. I quickly gave it back to the owner because I was afraid I would wreck it."

"That's easy to do with an airplane. I've flown one a couple of times. With the boats, if you stay away from the docks, it's pretty safe."

"In that case, I would love to try racing your boat. One race anyway."

The R/D called, "Boats in the water. We're going to try to finish the last nine heats without a rest stop."

All fourteen boats were in the water and ready to go within three minutes. They circled for one minute and then the next race was on. The nine races were finished quickly, with no stops, and the skippers pulled their boats out and started retuning them for the fun racing while waiting for the R/D to total the scores and announce the standings.

Finally he started calling out the finishing positions, beginning with number fourteen. Jim was called in fifth place and he said, "That's my best finish this season."

As the R/D was reading down the list, Bob and Mary were in deep discussion about sailing the boats, what other hobbies they had, where they liked to eat, and what siblings they had.

Finally the R/D yelled, "The number two finisher today is John."

At that Bob jumped three feet in the air, swinging his fist, and yelling, I won. I got first place."

The R/D called out, "Bob, come and get your first place trophy."

Bob looked at Mary and said, "You must be my good luck charm. This is the first time I have beaten John this year.

Mary started to blush, but Bob was still hopping around and didn't notice.

Bob finally settled down, turned to Mary and said, "We'll be getting the boats in the water in about five minutes. Let me show you how to control the boat. It just takes these two 'sticks'. One controls the rudder, the other controls the sail position. Going into the wind you want the sails pulled in, going away from the wind the sails should be all the way out. Controlling the rudder is fairly straight forward. I'll put the boat in the water and let you play with it a bit.

With the boat in the water Bob handed Mary the transmitter and she started to play with the controls, learning very quickly how to make the boat do what she wanted it to do.

"Boy, you are a quick learner. You're really smart, Mary."

"Well, I have a PhD in physics, if that can be taken as an indicator."

"We aren't too far apart. I have a Doctorate in psychology."

Mary didn't answer Bob, but she thought, t*he amazing part is that a psychologist can be that good at sailing, but I would never say that out loud.*

After five minutes Mary felt she understood fairly well how to control the boat. She knew, also, Bob would be standing right beside her ready to help.

The R/D said loudly, "Well. Let's get some fun sailing in, and remember boat number 863 is under the control of a beginner who will be getting help from Bob."

Without further comment he started the one-minute countdown to the start of the race. Mary just circled the boat, getting more used to the controls with twelve other boats in the water at the same time. The more she sailed the boat the more she understood how to control it.

At the start gun, Mary had the boat right at the middle of the line, with the other sailors giving her plenty of room.

With Bob's advice, Mary's boat hit the finish line in ninth place.

Bob said, "You did great. You really catch on quick."

In the fifth fun sail, Mary finished in fourth place with very little help from Bob and said, "I'm getting hungry. I think I will go to Doubleday's restaurant and get something to eat.

Bob replied, "Let me pack up my boat and I'll join you if you don't mind."

"Please do. I would like you to come along."

Bob hurriedly took his boat apart and packed it in his car. When he was done he asked, "Would you like to meet me at Doubleday's or ride with me there? Your car will be safe here until we get back."

Without any hesitation Mary said, "I'll ride with you, thank you."

As they drove along they had a lot of things to talk about, so the twenty minute drive seemed a lot shorter. At the restaurant they got a nice window booth and ordered their food. They continued talking like they had known each other for a long time.

After eating they headed back to get Mary's car. As they pulled into the parking lot, Mary asked, "How do I get an R/C boat like yours?"

Bob told her he knew of a couple for sale. He volunteered to go along with her to check them out. She said she would take him up on it.

Three days later Bob picked Mary up and they headed out to check the two boats. At the first stop, Bob took one look at the boat and said, "We'll think about it."

When they were back in the car, Bob said. That boat was not mighty yar. You wouldn't want it."

At the second stop, Bob looked at the boat and immediately said, "This boat looks good," He played with the electronics and saw everything worked great. "This boat seems to be mighty yar. I suggest you take it, Mary."

Mary paid for the boat, they packed it in the car, and took off. They then made a stop for lunch.

As they sat waiting for their food to come Mary asked, "You've mentioned 'mighty yar' and 'not mighty yar'. What does that really mean? I've never heard those expressions before."

"In boat talk 'mighty yar' means absolutely, perfectly, beautiful. There's no way to improve on it, or you in this case since I think you are mighty yar, also."

Mary blushed again and leaned over to kiss Bob on the cheek. Bob turned his head and wound up with a kiss on the mouth. They held the kiss for several seconds and then parted as the waiter brought their food.

One year later Bob and Mary were married. They lived happily ever after, raising a family of three kids and sailing R/C boats.

Printed in the United States
By Bookmasters